SUSAN LOWER

TRADE SECRETS

Time Glider
Books

Cover by Averi Hope Designs

Interior Design by Time Glider Books

ISBN: 978-1-945274-03-9

TRADE SECRETS

SUSAN LOWER

1

Milena Borghese paused at the front desk on her way out. "I'm headed out, Shauna. If anyone needs me, I'll be back in a few hours."

The young woman looked up from her phone. "Got it."

Milena shook her head and walked outside of Borghese Technology and waited for the car to pull up. A dark-skinned gentleman got out of the car and opened the door for her. "Good morning, Miss Borghese."

"Thank you. It's Benson, right?"

"Yes, Miss."

She got in the car. Sat her purse beside her and frowned at the message on her phone.

Locked out of the computer again. Need the password.

She shook her head, texting her father's protégé back.

You'll have to ask my father.

She curled her hand around the phone.

You were the last one in his office. I need those reports by later today.

"Nice try," she muttered. Reports? She'd seen someone

had tried to hack her father's mainframe. They were the one thing someone would go through that kind of trouble to get. Over her dead body. Her family's business had taken a hard enough hit these past few months with Boyko always one step ahead of them.

They had a leak with their company. It almost made her lose her appetite thinking of who would sell out their trade secrets to the highest bidder. Any of their competitors could bid on getting their hands on Borghese Technology's market share. But not f their security could sniff out the informant.

A pang of regret tapped into her feelings. Putting her phone back in her purse, Milena glanced out the window. "Benson? Where are you going? You should turn on Eastern Ave."

"There's an accident ahead. This way will still get you to your brunch on time "

Milena looked out the window. People were walking down the sidewalk. A man in slacks shoved his hands in his pockets, rocking back and forth at the crosswalk. A woman dug in her bag, not paying attention to the traffic or the lights blinking.

Milena's thoughts raced. Her fingers tightened over her purse straps. From the driver's seat, Benson glanced back at her through the rearview mirror. They sat at a red light. It wasn't so much she wanted to get to lunch with her mother, but she found it hard to stay still and not get out and walk.

Finding Ivan in her father's office earlier had unsettled her. "It will be shorter if I walk. You can circle and come back in about an hour. '

"I dare say I'd lose my job for doing that. No, thank you," Benson remarked.

"I assure you, me walking to lunch will be better for us both."

She scooted closer to the door. Her hand reached for the handle. The locks clicked.

The light turned green.

That unsettling feeling churned in her stomach.

Benson glanced again. The car turned instead of going straight.

Milena peered behind her. No sirens, no backed-up traffic.

Her grip tightened on her purse.

They turned on a side street. Milena pressed her hand to her stomach. "I'd prefer we stick to the main route."

The car pulled up. Parked.

On either side, the backs and sides of buildings. An air conditioner kicked on outside. Milena leaned back in her seat as Benson turned. "I'll be happy to let you out once you've given me the files for that project Mr. Yaroslav was after."

Benson held out his ebony hand.

"I don't know what you're talking about." Milena reached over, grabbed the lock, and tugged on it.

Benson took hold of her arm. "I'm sorry, Miss Borghese, but I need those files your father gave you. Many people are going to get hurt, including you, if you don't. I don't think either of us wants to see that happen."

"If these files are as important as you think they are, do you honestly believe I would remove them from the security of my father's office?"

Benson's brows drew together, and a frown formed on his face. "He said you'd have them. Give them to me. Now!"

"Who?" Instinctively she jerked her purse in front of her.

Benson's eyes widened. He went to reach for her purse, then paused. She turned her head to follow his gaze.

Suddenly, his head whipped around to look in front of them.

The sound of the car turning over, the awful screech of the starter as Benson turned it again as the car was already running. Milena looked ahead and gasped. She froze amid taking a breath. A man strode toward them from the front. He was dressed for business in a suit with a white shirt and a tie. His face covered from below the eyes with a scarf. The man lifted a gun. Pointed.

"Get—"

Milena jerked at the sound and slammed against the door. The lock released.

Benson's eyes stared at her in shock. His mouth slackened. He never got to finish what he wanted to say.

She tugged on the door again. The lever slipped through her hands. Something inside her pushed her forward. The door opened, and she fell out. Her exposed knees scraped on the asphalt. Biting her lip against crying out, she held onto her purse. Peering around the door, she spotted the man walking toward the car. Leisurely. His gun arm down. His face covered. His gaze locked on her.

Falling on her butt, she scrambled to get up. Staying behind the car door, she glanced around. Her heart thudded hard against her chest. The man continued forward, halfway between the front of the car and the end of the buildings. He raised his gun hand again, and she turned and ran.

Her heart pounded in her ears. She ran. She wobbled and twisted on her heels and took off. At the end of the alley, she turned and checked several back doors. Locked. By the grace of God, the fourth one opened. She burst into a tattoo shop. A man with a piercing in his brow looked up from working on another man's back. "Can I help you?"

She fought to catch her breath. Pulling back her shoulders, staying away from the instrument in his hand. She moved cautiously around him. "I need—" She wasn't sure what she needed. Would the man with the gun find her in here?

She gripped her purse.

"Chill, darlin'." The man with the piercing and skull tattoos down his arm flashed her an amused grin.

"Most people come through the front," a man sitting in a chair with his back bared muttered.

"She's nervous, Hal. Give her a moment."

The man with his back toward her swung his head around, looked at her through half-lidded eyes, and grunted.

"I get you're in a rush, but you'll have to wait a bit. I've got three more colors to add to Hal's back before I can help you," Tattoo guy said.

Milena never felt comfortable around needles. She nodded, hastened to get around them. She headed out of the tattoo parlor. To her left was a seating area with a couple of high-back chairs and a table with artwork. She moved around the seating, crouched down behind one chair, and wedged herself between the chair and the counter.

She heard Hal grunt again. The man with the tattoos said something, but she couldn't hear. Her heart was thundering in her ears. She searched through her purse, pulled out her phone.

She dialed, and her mother picked up on the third ring. "Milena, where are you? I'm sitting here alone."

"I'm not going to make it. I'm sorry, Mother."

Her mother huffed "You could have called earlier before I got here. Where are you? Ivan said you left to come to meet me."

"Something came up. I —"

She dropped the phone. It slid down and hit the floor, clattering on the tile and giving her the jitters. She tilted around the musty-smelling chair, glancing to the window. A man in dark suit pants paused looking inside. She leaned back, holding her breath.

Fumbling with the phone, she dug in her pocket. Finding the tiny fob, she attached it to her phone, searched through her downloads and told it to export. She slunk back against the wall.

Someone's cigarette butt ashes crushed beneath her hand. She bit her lip. Holding her breath, she watched the loading bar count from fourteen percent to twenty and counting.

The bell above the door rang. Every muscle in her body froze.

"Come back in a few hours, man. I can help you then," Tattoo guy shouted from the back.

She glanced down—thirty-four percent.

She clutched the phone to her chest.

On the other side of the chair, she heard someone's feet coming closer.

"Dude, I'm working here. What'cha need, bro?" Tattoo man had come to the counter. His head tilted and, for a second, she knew he had spotted her down behind the chair.

"Did a woman come in here?"

She knew that voice. It sent a chill to her bones.

"Whoa there. I don't work on anyone underage without consent. You feel me? Whoever you're looking for ain't got no business here."

Milena glanced up at the tattooed guy, his eyes narrowing, not looking at her.

Sixty-eight percent.

"Who you got in the back?"

"No one of your concern, buddy, and not a woman."

Milena's hands grew sweaty.

"I think I'll see for myself."

"And you'll let yourself out the back door," Tattoo guy said.

Sounds of boots on tiles, and Milena dared a peek up at the counter. Tattoo guy caught her gaze. He nodded and turned.

Ninety-six percent.

"Mind if I get back to my business now?"

The rear door shut. Tattoo man came walking out to the counter. He leaned over and stared down at her. "I don't know what you got going on, girl, but take it somewhere else."

Slowly, she rose. Slipping her purse strap over her shoulder and keeping the phone clutched in her other hand, Milena turned to tuck her hair back behind her ear.

"Thank you."

"I'd cross the street and go left if I were you." He winked and went back to Hal.

Milena peeked at the phone. Ninety-nine percent.

At the door, she took a deep breath. Her phone pinged. The phone hit one hundred percent. She pulled out the fob, tucked it in a place against her body where it would be safe. Outside on the street, she dropped the phone as she crossed between the traffic. A minivan ran over the device. She heard the crunch as she made it to the other side.

Ducking her head and pulling her hair to cover her face, Milena lengthened her stride, catching up with a group of people that cidn't notice her in all their chatting. She stayed close to the buildings until she spotted her opportunity and turnec left.

Soon she caught up with others walking and tried to blend in.

———

Twelve fifty-nine. Nash Dunford stared at his watch for a solid minute, willing it to turn over on the hour. He gave up his lunch to gain more time. For the past eight months, he labored along with the roofing crew to make a day's wage. He owed his younger brother for hooking him up after his last job had ended in a flat dismissal.

It had been a matter of time after he shot his mouth off to the boss's daughter. Another he added to his list of keeping his nose clean. Don't fall for the boss's daughter. Better yet—and this was the one that had been the clincher —don't share your theories of corruption unless you can prove them.

It soured his gut still.

He watched the time turn and reached for his lunch cooler. He couldn't wait to get off this hot roof and sit in his recliner for the rest of the afternoon.

Nash moved toward the ladder at the side of the two-story office building, spotted an Orioles cap atop the head of a man coming up. He stepped back, waiting for his turn.

"Don't tell me you're headed home?"

Nash grinned. "My job is down here for the day. I leave the flashing all to you."

Chuck, one of the men on his roofing crew, threw back his head and laughed. Nash held out his hand to help Chuck the rest of the way up on the roof.

"Around the chimney? Man, you got to leave your shirt on."

Nash rolled back his shoulders before unbuckling his tool belt, hooked the handle of his lunch cooler to his side, and fastened it again.

"As long as the Orioles win today." Nash couldn't wait to get home. The game and his recliner awaited him. He deserved an afternoon off.

He worked ten-hour days trying to prove himself. Good-paying jobs weren't easy to find. Not when your last employer tainted your name in the hiring pool.

All he needed was an afternoon, his Orioles, and a cold drink to dissolve another fraction of bitterness he carried. He'd like to let it go entirely, but then he'd have to stop thinking of the woman he lost his job over.

Wiping his hands down his pants to absorb the sweat, he grabbed the ladder. "Enjoy your afternoon."

Chuck shook his head. Nash could imagine all the dirty words Chuck was calling him right this instant in his head. "I hope they lose."

"I'm sure you do. Don't let me keep you from that flashing." Nash hurried to swing onto the ladder and make his way down before Chuck got it in his head to shake the ladder or try to keep him from going down. He could be funny. But there was nothing funny about falling two stories or having to work out in this blasted blistering sun all day.

Summer hadn't hit the calendar by far, but hot tar on any day sapped the energy out of a man.

They would have the roof finished by tomorrow and no one on the street would know they'd been there. Life in Baltimore would go on, people on the sidewalks, business as usual, and Nash left, nursing old blisters, waiting for them to heal.

Down the street, sirens screamed. He paid enough attention to make sure they wouldn't interfere with his ride home. The game called him. One of these days, he'd get tickets. But for today, he'd watch it on the big screen. His feet propped up. The Orioles were coming home.

Oh yeah.

His phone pinged, and he pulled it from his pocket.

Don't forget to pick up the pizza.

At his truck, he took off his tool belt and tossed it in on the seat. His lunch cooler rolled down and pulled the leather belt to the floorboards. Getting the truck started and the air conditioning blaring, he reached beneath him, felt the warm metal, and headed home.

He pulled up at a red light. Directly in front of him, on the other side of the intersection, a black Mercedes sat, its driver watching the rearview more than the light.

But that wasn't what caught Nash's attention. He rode in a car like that not long ago. If the back passenger was as beautiful as the woman who flittered in his mind, he wouldn't pay attention to waiting on the light either.

But even if it was the same car, it was a different driver.

The light changed, and Nash watched the car turn. A horn sounded, bringing Nash's mind back to picking up the pizza, getting home, and getting ready for the game to come on.

2

She should have called first.

She had only been to this place a few times. Without her driver, Milena had no sense of direction. She should have paid more attention to where she was going all those times than to the man who had driven her there.

At the very least, she should have put Nash's address in her phone or committed more than the street name to memory.

All the houses on the street looked too much alike.

What if he got a different car or moved to a different neighborhood? She hitched her purse strap more securely over her shoulder and tried not to look too obvious as she glanced behind her.

The back of her legs ached, and her feet screamed that the designer pair of heels she wore weren't made for walking miles through the city.

She'd lost track of the time. All the places she passed and all the street names remained a blur. She held onto her purse to keep her hands from shaking.

Hopefully, she'd remember the right section of town. She couldn't risk taking any kind of transportation. Even as the sun hit its high point, someone was looking for her.

Relief came at the sight of a blue truck parked in the driveway.

It had been almost a year since Nash had tried to warn her about her father's secret dealings, and she'd refused to believe him. She'd taken her father's side out of love and loyalty

If only she'd trusted Nash, she might not be in this mess.

He hadn't even tried to see her again once she'd told him to stay away from her. And it hurt.

Milena's heel caught the edge of the uneven sidewalk, and she tripped, her ankle going to the side, and she caught herself. Leaning into a car, the alarm went off, and her heart took off in a panic.

Dogs barked from the backyard of the house she just passed. Her anxiety skyrocketed.

It took everything she had not to run down the sidewalk and up the stairs to the house with the black garage door.

Someone shouted at the dogs, and a few moments later, the car alarm went silent.

Milena listened to her heart thudding in her chest.

She pressed the doorbell.

A year was a long time to show up and admit you were wrong.

Please be home. Please be home. She glanced behind her.

A car turned down the street. A dark SUV headed, slowly, in her direction.

She knocked, frantic to get inside, no matter if she'd gotten the right house or not.

Could she handle seeing him with someone else?

Trust me, Mila. I would never lie to you.

The hope that he would accept her apology and forgive her kept her feet planted at his front door.

She heard movement inside. She shifted all her weight on her good ankle. She clutched the strap of her purse, not wanting to look too desperate. Her breath held in her lungs as the knob turned.

Milena hadn't thought it through any further than finding him. Maybe this hadn't been a good idea.

She turned to go away, paused at the step. Where had the dark SUV gone?

"Milena."

So she'd found the right house.

She pulled back her shoulders, tried to steady her nerves to face him again. Turning, her stomach wavered.

"Nash."

His broad shoulder leaned against the doorway, blocking her view inside. He held the door, those arms, bulging with muscle against his short sleeves as he held the door, ready to slam it in her face any minute.

He'd been hitting the gym more than when she'd last seen him. Those cynical eyes hardened at the sight of her.

"What are you doing here?"

"Can I come in?" She glanced over her shoulder. The SUV had parked on the opposite side of the road, a few houses down. A woman got out and walked around to the back.

"Milena."

She turned her attention back to him. In their time together, he hadn't ever used her full name. It stung, along with his icy tone, more than she wanted to admit.

The six months they'd had together seemed nonexistent.

He towered over her. His six-foot-two height was drawn up in full, but she wouldn't let him intimidate her.

"You wanted to come in?" He held the door open, stepping back for her to enter, his voice hard, like his eyes, and not at all welcoming.

With no other choice, she went inside.

She jumped at the sound of the door closing. "I never thought I'd find you on my doorstep."

His admission struck her worse than the day's events.

She questioned her sanity for coming here. Maybe waiting for the police and going to them would have been better.

She'd always been able to trust him. Until she hadn't.

Truth squeezed the confidence from her.

She couldn't force him to help her. If someone followed her here, then she was putting him in danger, too. Would he think that had been her intent all along?

He left her in the foyer. Taking a moment, she slipped out of her torturous heels. She checked to make sure the door was locked.

Inside the living room, a woman rose from the couch. A woman wearing an oversized sweater, with two-toned brown hair pulled up in a messy bun.

A guy walked down the hall, a bowl of popcorn and drinks in his hands. "Hey, you didn't say you'd invited someone else to watch the game with us."

"I didn't," Nash said.

"I'm sorry. I've come at an awful time. I can come back another time if that is better." Her manners would get her killed.

"What are you doing here, Milena?"

"I need to speak with you. Alone." She glanced at the other two. Already, she had put them all in danger.

"Where is your driver?" Nash crossed his arms.

"He's dead."

———

Poor Bryon almost dropped the popcorn in Jaylene's lap. Nash took Milena by the arm and pulled her into the kitchen. "When did this happen?"

"A few hours ago," she confessed.

Her father had made it very clear he wouldn't work in this town or any other if he went anywhere near her.

"How did it happen?"

"They killed him."

"Who?"

"The men who are after me."

"Explain."

"I'm sorry, Nash. I should have trusted you."

They could get to that later. All he wanted was to know what happened.

She sank into a chair at the kitchen island. A bruise on her cheek, below her right eye, and a scratch on her chin drew his attention. Her skittish demeanor set off a silent alarm, unsettling him. Startling him.

He touched her cheek, careful of her tender flesh. Told himself he needed to make sure this was real. She was real. Gently, his fingers barely touched her face.

The wariness in her eyes evaporated. It drew the tension from inside him, held him together a bit more.

He couldn't help it. Despite the doubts and the good of his own conscience warning him that his actions would lead to more trouble. He leaned in.

Her lips parted.

"The game's about to start!" Bryon shouted.

The moment lost by the return of icy fear in her eyes. Nash's hand fell to his side, and he pulled back.

"Be there in a second." His kid brother and his brother's girlfriend would have to watch the game without him. The Twins were playing the Orioles.

"You've got five minutes while they sing the anthem." He looked at his watch. He would have to make it enough time.

"You were right about my father."

"You said that."

"I don't know everything that's going on. One moment I'm headed downtown for brunch, and the next I noticed we aren't going the right direction. When I asked to get out and walk, Benson pulled over and demanded I give him files. He didn't specify what files, but I have a feeling he wanted the ones on our latest development."

"What happened to Carlos?" Nash asked.

"How am I supposed to know? It's not my job to keep track of drivers."

Nash gave a wave of his hand. "Go on."

She took a second to regain her composure. "A man walked toward the car. He pulled out a gun and shot Benson."

He could see the flash of fear in her eyes. In all the months they'd been apart he hadn't stopped thinking of her, stopped praying for her. His feelings hadn't changed for her. Nash wanted to assure her that she was safe with him, but he had to know what happened.

"Then?" he prompted, softly.

She breathed in deep, struggling to find words. "I ran. I jumped out onto the sidewalk and ran. I hid in a tattoo shop and then worked myself into the center of a group of people walking and chatting down the street. I followed them into a café, and then I waited as long as I could before heading here. I believe the man who shot my driver is after me, too."

"You gave him the slip?"

"The best I could. I remember what you told me. I kept moving. I didn't wait for him to find me. He came into the tattoo shop. I ditched my phone on the other side of town."

No one could track her. She had been listening to him. Not enough for her to trust him.

"Police?"

"I came here."

He scratched his chin. "We should call the authorities. They might be looking for you. Someone would have seen what happened."

"I don't know. I didn't think. I just ran." Horror marred her beautiful face. Her thick black hair hung down her back, and her eyes dulled with shock and fear.

He took her by the arms. "You are a witness to a crime, Milena. Someone could have seen you running away, and the police might be out looking for you."

"Me?" She paled. "They'll think I did it."

"Maybe." He pulled her into his arms.

Bryon came down the hallway. "Everything okay?"

"I need to make some calls. Mila, this is my brother, Bryon."

"The chick that got you fired." Bryon crossed his arms.

"Fired?" Milena pulled back from him.

"We'll talk about it later. Mila is in trouble and needs our protection right now."

"So, you're going to work for her again?" Bryon asked.

His brother raised his brows at Nash, and he didn't have the time for it. He needed to talk to the cops and find out if Milena was on the suspect list.

He had tried to warn her it was only a matter of time before her father's dealings put her in danger. Did she know? He always suspected she might. Especially after the way her father fired him, and she ignored his attempts to see her.

"Something like that," he muttered.

As he punched in the number for the police station, Jaylene came down the hall. "A guy is coming up on the porch. It's like Men in Black out there."

She hitched her thumb toward the door.

Nash's video surveillance notified him on his phone as soon as the man stepped on the porch. He turned the face of his phone around. "Recognize this guy?"

Milena went white. She nodded. "He's —"

Nash moved down the hall. "Jaylene, you take Milena upstairs. They'll have the house covered. Bryon, you watch the back."

"So much for watching the game." Bryon pushed past Milena and scowled at her. Jaylene grabbed Milena by the hand, pulled her to the staircase, and headed upstairs. Once the women were out of sight, Nash walked to the door, waited for the sound of the doorbell.

He glanced back—Bryon had moved out of sight—and Nash pulled open a drawer of the bureau by the stairs. He tucked the handgun in his waistband behind his back.

Slowly, he opened the door. "Can I help you?"

The man in the black suit narrowed his eyes on Nash. "You will let Miss Borghese know her car is waiting."

Parked on the street, a black SUV sat.

Nash went with his gut instincts. "I think you've got the wrong address."

Nash closed the door. The man grabbed the door. In his

unusual accent, he said, "I think you should send Miss Borghese out. My patience are few."

"And so are mine." Nash's gaze fell to the man's hand on the door. "I'd let go if I were you."

"It is imperative Miss Borghese comes with me."

"Good luck in finding her."

Nash slammed the door, the man letting go before it smashed his hand. He locked the door, leaned back against it, and watched from the security app on his phone as the man straightened his suit and stepped off the porch.

The man got in the car and appeared to pull out a phone and call someone. A few minutes later, the car pulled away from the house.

In the other room, he heard the blare from the television where the game went on without him.

3

"We'll need to get you some clothes and a disguise to get you out of here. They'll be watching the place." Nash walked into the bedroom where Milena sat between the bed and the wall, hiding.

Slowly she rose, tugging on her dress, suddenly feeling more self-conscious under his stare.

"How do we get out of here? I'm sorry, Nash. I didn't know they followed me."

"I called Gina. Once she gets here, we'll figure it out." Nash walked back out of the room.

"Who's Gina?" Milena asked.

Jaylene gave her a sympathetic smile. "She's on the police force. Nash's been dating her off and on for a few months."

The man had a right to move on. It didn't matter, anyway. She might not live long enough to think about happily-ever-afters. Nash deserved to have someone in his life. Someone who would trust him.

"Bryon mentioned you. Nash used to work for your father, right?" Jaylene asked.

"My father owns Borghese Technology. Before Nash left, he was head of the company security."

"You mean before your father fired him," Jaylene said.

"It was my understanding Nash quit." It was the second time she had heard about it. After knowing what she now knew of her father, she wouldn't put it past him. No wonder Nash hadn't ever tried to get in touch with her all this time. Had her father threatened him?

"So you're dating his younger brother?" Changing the subject seemed like a safer option for both of them.

"We've known each other since high school." Jaylene shrugged. "We got together after his last tour in Afghanistan. We're both Orioles fans."

"If I remember correctly, Nash has a fondness for sports."

Jaylene snorted and laughed. "You think?"

She waved her hand. "You might as well clean up. Gina will have fresh clothes, and if she doesn't, I have an overnight bag in my car I can get you. We're about the same size."

"That would be lovely," Milena said.

Jaylene gave her an odd look, then pointed. "You can use the guest bathroom there."

Something about stripping off her clothes and using Nash's bathroom made her feel vulnerable and unsure about herself. While the thought of washing off the sweat and the other lingering residue of the day's events tempted her, Milena needed to talk to Nash first.

She had a friend in Florida who had invited her to come visit if she could find a way to the airport and get on a plane. It would put distance between her and the men following her.

Think, Milena. Think.

She had gotten herself into this mess. She would have to figure out how to get out of it. Maybe going straight to the police would have been a better option.

They would have found her first.

She headed downstairs. Speaking to Nash was the most urgent task on her agenda.

In the living room, the television played with no one in the room. Further down the hall, in the kitchen, she heard Nash's voice.

"You should take Jaylene home. Stay there."

"You shouldn't get involved. Once Gina gets here, hand her over and wash your hands of this," Bryon said.

"She acted as if she didn't know they had fired you," Jaylene said.

"She might not have," Nash's voice trailed off.

"You shouldn't get involved with her again," Bryon said.

Milena hated to eavesdrop. She moved toward the kitchen when Nash and a woman came through the back door. She had a badge on her hip and wore a uniform. Her pixie cut blonde hair and manicured nails made her appear more feminine than tough.

Looks could be deceiving.

Milena had found that out the hard way.

Nash wrapped an arm around the woman, and she kissed him. Not at all the friendly peck on the cheek, but the kind that said they'd had more than the few occasional dates Jaylene had mentioned.

She looked away while trying to gather the courage to meet her replacement.

"Is this her?"

"I thought you were taking a shower." Jaylene crossed her arms.

Lost for words, Milena pulled back all her fleeting emotions.

"I'm Gina. You must be Milena." Gina walked up to her, held out her hand. "I understand you have a situation."

One Milena hadn't realized would pull so many other people into her life at once.

"My driver Benson—"

"Nash told me. Listen, we didn't find any shootings reported or abandoned cars with broken windshields."

"It would have been by Thames Street Oyster House."

"I'll call it in, but I think someone would have reported it by now."

Milena's stomach sank.

"I'll need you to come down to the station, fill out a report, and answer a few questions."

Milena shook her head. "I can't."

"Do you know who the man was?"

Milena's heart sank with her stomach. He'd told her everything. Rightly so, but it meant he trusted this Gina more than her.

"I'm not sure." Her hands shook again. "His face was covered, but he wore a business suit."

Gina squeezed her hand. "Violent crimes often upset people. Why don't you get freshened up, and we'll get you down to the precinct where you'll be safe to give your statement?"

Milena glanced around at all their faces. All of them appeared eager to get rid of her. She swallowed back regret and apology. Nash's eyes had turned suspicious.

"Is it possible your father could have sent those men out of concern for your whereabouts?"

"No."

"He could have someone keeping an eye on you," Nash said.

Someone who watched over her and protected her just like Nash?

"I can assure you he doesn't."

"That doesn't sound like your father," Nash said.

"Says the man who tried to convince me otherwise," Milena pointed out.

"Think you can be ready to go in fifteen?" Gina asked, handing her a bag of clothes.

Upstairs, Milena washed and freshened up. None of the clothes Gina brought fit Milena's curvy figure. Keeping her prior outfit, she pulled her hair up into a messy bun, slid and secured the fob in a not-so-prominent place.

In the hall, she could hear their voices as she approached the stairs.

Big mistake, Milena. She promised not to let eavesdropping become a habit.

"There's no vehicle behind or around the restaurant, no witnesses, and no body." Gina's voice floated up the stairs.

"Doesn't mean it didn't happen," Nash said.

"She could be the one who killed him," Gina countered. "You need to stay here while I take her in."

Take her in?

No, Milena stepped back inside the guest room. She had to find out what happened to Benson. And that man. The one who chased her. Who was he working for? And he wasn't alone. A cramp formed in her belly. She couldn't take the blame for another man's crime.

Outside the window of the guest bedroom, she searched

for signs of the men or the car. Under her breath, she muttered a quick prayer for Benson. No matter what the man had done, no one deserved to have their life taken away. He should have justice and his family closure. And no way would she allow thoughts of guilt to trickle in her mind. Benson could have let her out of the car.

He could have taken the usual route as she asked.

Her heart slowed a little. It beat at a fast pace for so long that, when it lessened, she had to take a deep breath. Nash's girlfriend wanted to take her downtown. She couldn't end up like Benson.

She should have grabbed a cheap prepaid phone and called... who? Alysa? Her mother? Her father? Ivan? Her head hurt. She had to get out of here while she had the chance.

A knock came on the closed door.

"You okay in there?"

Slowly, she pulled up the window. "Yes. I'll meet you downstairs in a few minutes."

She'd taken enough gymnastic lessons in her youth that slipping out the window and landing on the back porch roof in her bare feet wasn't tricky. Her purse strap positioned across her chest, and her shoes dangling in her hand, she moved over to the far corner of the porch. She trembled the closer she came to the edge.

Coming to Nash had been a long shot. Panic had caused a lapse in her judgment. He was the first person who came to her mind for help. *You can always trust me.* Clearly, she'd lost her mind. Why else would she have thought of Nash after all this time?

He hadn't cared enough about her back then to stick around, and she'd been wise not to believe him.

Or his meter maid girlfriend.

The only option she had left was to take her friend Alysa up on her offer to join her in Miami.

It would buy her some time.

She could get a flight out of Baltimore and call Alysa once she landed.

After she had the fob secured and the new device launched, this would all end. In. About. A. Year. Could she protect it that long? Or until her father returned, and they had another way to keep the device's blueprint out of their competitor's hands.

Stop thinking about business and start thinking about living.

Milena took a deep breath, looked down at the ground. Ten feet at most. Her father and the government better thank her for this.

"Milena!" Nash leaned out the window.

Startled, her heart stuck in her throat. Milena jumped and rolled, stunned at first, then gathered her shoes and took off in a flat run. Shouts from inside the house couldn't stop her. She ran.

She'd always been an excellent runner. Better if she had running shoes.

Nash's backyard didn't have a fence, and Milena took off through the next yard and the next. She rushed across another street and paid no attention to the hard pavement under her bare feet.

She ducked and moved around the awning of someone's backyard and hid behind a set of garbage cans to catch her breath.

She'd been a fool to trust Nash, but desperation had forced her to take a chance. That and the voice in her heart whispered for an excuse to see him again. And she'd deny the latter if ever she needed to confess.

Nash slammed his fist on the windowsill. His phone had sent an alert that someone had messed with the window.

He hurried down the hall, descended the stairs where Gina waited. "Where is she?"

Jaylene and Bryon peered out from the living room. Jaylene's gaze went back to the game, and Bryon got up. "Now what?"

"Milena's gone. She slipped out the window."

"From upstairs?" Jaylene asked.

Bryon turned off the television and rose. "Looks like none of us are watching a game today. I warned you she was trouble."

"She's going to get herself killed," Nash said.

"Why would she run?" Jaylene asked. "Didn't she come to you for help?"

Nash ran his hand through his hair. "I don't know."

Unless she wasn't telling the truth.

Unless there was something more going on.

Unless she didn't trust him.

Trust me, Mila. Trust me now.

Gina gave him a sidelong glance. "You call and tell me your ex shows up and needs help, then she takes off. Are you sure she's not the one who killed the guy?"

"Mila wouldn't hurt a fly."

What made her run?

Gina had gone to check on her.

He should have given her more time to calm down before calling for reinforcements.

"I'm going to look for her," Nash said.

"Which way do you want me to go?" Bryon tossed the remote in his hand on the couch.

Jaylene sat frowning at them.

"I'm calling this in," Gina said.

"Calling what?" Nash threw up his hand. Every second he delayed, Milena could be further out of his reach.

"You said you didn't find a body. No body. No crime."

"She's hiding something," Gina said.

"She's scared. Something spooked her," Nash said.

"This is turning into a police investigation. You need to stay clear of it," Gina warned.

"She came to me because she was in trouble. I have to find her."

"Any idea where she'd go?" Bryon interrupted.

Nash tried to think. It had been a long time, and things had most definitely changed between them. "I have a few ideas. You take the south section. She might head to Riverside."

"She won't get far on foot," Gina pointed out.

"Milena is resourceful. I wouldn't underestimate what she's capable of." Nash headed for the door.

Gina laid her hand on his arm. "You're a good guy, Nash. I don't want to see you get hurt."

"I'll call when I find her."

"Remember, you need to let the authorities handle this." Gina squeezed his arm. He dodged having her come closer. They'd gone out a few times, and they both agreed they worked better together as friends.

Although the kiss she'd landed on him in front of Milena had felt possessive.

The first place he went was the backyard and then started jogging in the direction he'd seen her go.

Where else would she be going?

He heard a dog bark and followed the sound. Spotting a figure dashing across a lawn, he ran after them. Another street over, he found where she'd dropped a shoe, but he was closing in on her.

When he scooped up the shoe, he lost sight of her and came to a halt in a development full of minivans and family homes. Slowly, he walked across the lawn to get back to the sidewalk. At the corner, a black car drove down the street. Nash recognized the car from earlier.

So, the man her father sent was still looking for her.

Whatever mess she'd gotten into, she'd come to him for help, and Nash had let her down. Maybe a part of him had called Gina to show Milena he hadn't waited around for her.

"Nice going," Nash muttered, glancing around, searching for the woman he had scared away.

He had a habit of dropping things on her too soon, and this time it might have driven her deeper into danger. Whatever disappointment he held from her not trusting him the first time, he would have to let it go.

She was the one who showed up on his doorstep after all these months. Some things were worth waiting for.

And he was about to lose it if he couldn't find her before the black car got to her first.

Nash held onto her shoe, listening and looking for any other signs of her. He moved between the houses, since most people were at work and kids were in school. Unless they'd gotten off at lunch and come home to watch the Orioles and the Twins play. You couldn't live in Baltimore and not be an Orioles or Ravens fan.

He spotted her black hair and saw her foot sticking out from around a trash can. An adolescent boy stood close to where she huddled close to the green bins and stared at her.

A moment later, the boy's mother called him, and he

ran back to her. The boy pointed, and Milena took off again.

"Gotcha." This time, he took off in a full sprint. The black car rolled onto the street, and she veered to the left, through another yard.

"Mila, stop! Wait!" He had to get her before she ran across the street, right into the view of the black car.

She glanced back at him, about to burst out onto the street. Nash shoved her onto the ground behind a row of trimmed hedges.

He knocked the wind from her, keeping her on her back as he covered and watched for the black car to continue down the street. Recovering quickly, Milena shoved against him. "Get off me. Let me go!"

"Quiet!" He put his hand on over her mouth and pressed even closer atop her. Her breath came in hot pants against his palm. It was hard for him to ignore the way her chest heaved to catch her breath. He gritted his teeth, watched, and waited.

Her tongue darted out of her mouth and licked his hand. He jerked it back. "Seriously?" he whispered.

She glared at him. "Let. Me. Go."

"Fine." He eased back enough to give her more space. "But your friends are coming down the street. If you run now, you'll catch them."

Her face drained of color, and she slumped back against the ground. "That's what I thought."

She rolled over on her stomach, parted the bush, and they both peered through.

Mindful of where his hands were, Nash kept her trapped in his arms as he hovered above her, looking out. He had dropped the shoe as soon as he caught her.

He noticed the other shoe over by the trash, but more so, the black car passed them and went down the street.

Nash pulled back, sat close to her as she pulled up on her knees. "Now that they're gone, mind telling me why you jumped out of my window?"

Milena smoothed down the front of her dress. "Because I woke up this morning and decided I needed a little more adventure in my life. You know, go to the office, have an early lunch, almost get killed, and get accused of committing a crime that no one seems to think existed, but that I'm apparently guilty of just the same."

She huffed, reaching over and snatching her shoe from where it laid. He reached overhand, grabbed the other. "No one is accusing you of anything."

"Are you sure about that?" She reached over and plucked the shoe from his hand. "I thought you of all people would understand and help me. You were the one who came to me all those months ago and accused my father of blackmailing to get contracts."

Grabbing the shoe put them both off balance. Nash fell back, and Milena fell atop him. His arm went around her. "I do understand." Or he had tried.

He spent months trying to find proof for her to believe him. Borghese Technology had doubled their security after they fired him and made sure he couldn't get within a hundred yards of the place.

"Do you mind?" She struggled to get out of his hold.

Not that he wouldn't mind holding onto her a little longer. Nash said, "On one condition."

Milena rolled her eyes. "And what is that?"

"You're straight with me from here on out."

"Are you implying I've been lying to you?"

"You don't trust me."

When she didn't answer, he squeezed his arm around her tighter. "Whatever is going on, we'll figure it out together."

And a little intervention from God couldn't hurt either. He had let Milena walk away from him once, and when the time came, she would walk away from him again. The choice was never his to make.

"Fine, but I'd prefer it if we can keep your girlfriend out of this."

"Gina?" Nash didn't have time to go into any other details. He spotted his truck the next street over. Jumping to his feet and pulling her with him, Nash tugged her in that direction. "Come on, before they head this way again."

Nash scanned the street before stepping out and flagging down his brother.

"Bryon, I thought you were going south."

"Gina went that way, she called it into the station, and they've put out an APB on her."

Nash ran his hand through his hair. "I'll take care of it. First, I'll drop you back at the house with Jaylene."

Bryon got out of the truck and went around to the other side. Nash helped Milena in, waited for her to move to the middle, and got behind the steering wheel.

"Jay's freaking out about this," Bryon said.

"She'll have to get used to it if she's going to marry a guy in the security business," Nash said.

His brother had proposed a few months ago, and their parents were driving in from Virginia in a few weeks for the engagement party.

He stopped at the house long enough to drop Bryon off, and Milena slid further away from him in the truck. It might have been miles for the way she kept her gaze fixed on Bryon's back until he disappeared in the house.

She came to him.

There was still hope.

He turned the truck around and started driving. Her shoes lay by her feet, but she hadn't put them on.

"Why did you run?" Nash's grip on the steering wheel tightened. He wasn't about to let this go.

4

"I thought I made it clear. I came to you for help. Then you called your girlfriend and tried to wash your hands of me."

"I called Gina to help, and she's not my girlfriend."

It didn't matter. What mattered was she couldn't trust Nash. She needed to keep the secrets on the fob she possessed safe; otherwise, fallen into the wrong hands, her father's competitors could use the technology blueprints to build their own devices. This one wasn't for commercial use. If a terrorist group in her parents' homeland of Russia got their hands on it, the world wouldn't be safe. People got annoyed, thinking cameras spied on them everywhere. How about a listening device in your phone?

Oh, no. She couldn't let this device fall into the wrong hands. She'd been three when they came to America, and, while her parents never told her, she suspected their departure had to do with one of her father's inventions.

Even if she tried to explain this to the police, they wouldn't believe her, and she would break about half the requirements in the contract with the United States government's agency. She wasn't sure she could contact the government agency since they dealt with her father on these matters. It would take a lot of faith on the police's part to believe her when she could be in bigger trouble with the FBI for discussing government secrets. She hoped Nash, of all people, would see the truth in her story.

"She thinks I killed someone and hid the body," Milena said.

"You heard that?"

Milena made a sound in her throat, annoyed.

"You still live on Harborview?"

"Yes."

"I'll swing by the police station first. You can give them your statement, and then I'll take you home."

"Is that where your girlfriend is meeting you?" she asked, with a little too much bitterness. It wasn't as if Nash had ever kissed her the way she saw Gina kiss him. Not at all the sweet, peck-on-the-cheek kind of friendship kiss he gave her long ago.

She touched her cheek, tried not to dwell on it.

He moved on. And so would she.

She needed to focus on keeping Borghese's technology out of the wrong hands and staying alive.

"Gina and I are friends, nothing more," Nash said, his jaw clenching as he continued to drive.

"I'm sure she'll be happy to see you either way after you drop me off at home."

"You mean the police station."

Milena looked at him. "Home. Please. I would prefer a change of clothes and more appropriate footwear before I'm locked up."

"They're not going to lock you up," Nash said.

"Says the man whose girlfriend is trying to put me away for a crime which no one believes happened."

"It's not like that."

"If you say. Now, home, if you please." She spoke to him as she would her father's driver. Not caring that his forehead wrinkled, and that tic returned to the muscle in his jaw. There was more at risk than Nash's feelings.

Never once had he considered hers. Why else would he drop volatile information in her lap and leave her all those months ago?

The rest of the drive was quiet. Most of the houses in the row looked the same. Blue hydrangea and boxwood shrubs hugged front entrances. Once they parked in the drive of her condominium, Milena reached for the handle of the door. Nash hit the button on his door to lock it.

"I'm going inside with you." His hard stare said he wouldn't take no for an answer.

"I hope you don't expect me to make you coffee afterward." She pulled the lock mechanism and got out. Across the street, a dog barked, and Milena fished for her house keys in her purse. Mostly, everyone on this part of the street stuck to themselves. She knew little about the people or the names of those who lived around here.

Making a plan in her head to change clothes, grab a travel bag, and her passport just in case, she paused.

Nash came up behind her. "In a hurry this morning?"

Her grip on her keys tightened. She bit her lip as Nash pushed the door the rest of the way open.

Too stunned to step inside, Milena stood there while Nash entered. When she left this morning, her house had been tidy and neat.

Someone had been here.

They sorted through her closets and drawers, emptying

their contents on the floor. In the kitchen, the refrigerator kicked on. They'd left the door open after searching in there, too.

A foreboding ache gnawed at her stomach. They could still be inside.

"Nash," she whispered.

He glanced back at her. "Stay here. Call the cops."

Nash reached behind him, pulled out his handgun, and stepped over the tossed couch cushions to go into the next room. Milena stepped through the doorway, moving off to the side. She leaned back against the wall, tilted her head to listen for anyone upstairs.

She moved when Nash passed her, went up the stairs, and she followed. After he'd gone into each of the two bedrooms, her office, and both bathrooms, she sighed.

"I thought I told you to stay put."

"There is no one here." Someone wanted those files. Who?

"But you knew that." He put his gun away.

"No, Nash. Despite what your girlfriend at the police station might think, I'm not a slob to leave my house this way. It is disappointing you would think so little of my home organization skills."

She walked into her bedroom, not caring that he followed her. Tipping over a photo of them together before he could spot it, she kept her hand on it to steady her nerves. There were two people, other than herself, who had a key to get in her apartment.

"Did you call the cops?"

"With what? You know I ditched my phone."

They had purged her bedroom closet, too. They ripped her bedsheets from her bed. And even the dresser drawers dangled from the frame with the contents spilled.

A tiny sob swelled in Milena as she knelt on the carpet. She swallowed it down, picking up her unmentionables, and stuffed them back in a drawer, grateful Nash wasn't paying attention. The last thing she wanted him seeing was her black lace underthings. A girl had to have some secrets.

She heard him on his phone.

"Yeah, I found her. We're at her place. It's trashed." He paused, his eyes on her.

Milena could feel them boring into her back as she searched for her small suitcase.

"Touch nothing until the police get here," Nash said, then went back to his conversation. "I'll check it for forced entry. It was open when we got here."

By the casual way he spoke, she knew he had called Gina.

He nodded, and Milena ignored him. The police would show up soon, and she needed to collect her things. Inside her closet, she bumped the secret panel of her safe. Nash leaned against the doorjamb of the walk-in wardrobe.

She pulled out her passport, some cash, and locked it back up. "If you would kindly step out, I need to change and pack."

She realized she'd left her shoes in Nash's truck.

"What kind of game is this, Milena?"

"Is that what you think this is?" That hurt. A lot.

"Gina says there is a missing persons report filed on you. A guy named Ivan Yaroslav. Who is he?"

Milena sank down on the corner of the misshapen boxspring of her bed. The mattress was flipped and leaning against her bed stand.

"Ivan Yaroslav is—" She searched for the best way to describe her relationship with Ivan. It was a business deal, so therefore she said, "Ivan is my father's business associate.

He's not looking for me. Not exactly. He wants the plans to the communication tracker device our company has been developing."

"If your father made a deal with him, why not give him the device?" Nash asked.

"My father left for Russia over a week ago for business. He wouldn't say what for, but he didn't take my mother with him. They usually always travel together. While he is away, my father left Ivan in charge. I overheard him a few days ago speaking with one of our investors."

"That's good, right?"

Milena shook her head. "I heard him mention the Telek. My father would have never mentioned a top-secret contract to Ivan. He wouldn't have wanted Ivan's family to know the depth of our business, Nash. We're dealing with a government contract, not your local cell service provider."

Why did she ever think she could explain this to him? He understood security systems and locked doors. Surely, the man understood the measures they went through to keep their designs from falling into the wrong hands. He was a security guard. It was his job to secure and protect. And once upon a time, securing and protecting her father's assets had been his job. Until the day it wasn't.

"So, this Telek is what your driver was after, and you think Yaroslav is, too?"

She could see what he was thinking, and he wouldn't entirely be wrong. "Yes."

"Ivan is planning on taking over the company and all the technology. His family has been blackmailing my father for years. This is the one thing my father has kept from him. It makes sense. When I found him in my father's office this morning, he was looking for something. He asked me about the computer's password. Then later, Benson asked me for the files. Ivan would have had to put him up to it. How else would he know about it?"

Nash scratched his chin, so she went on. "Ivan would want to make sure my father isn't cutting him out of the deal. His family would want insurance that my father isn't going back on an old debt. No matter the cost, the Telek can't fall into the retail market."

"This is all about one of your father's trade secrets getting leaked?" Nash put his hands on his hips.

"My father's company employs workers here and in Russia. You were right about my father's side deals, but I don't think he was the one orchestrating them. I knew he had private dealings with several government agencies, but I looked into it after you left. While my father might have been aware of what was happening, I believe it has been Ivan controlling things for a while."

"And this has to do with Yaroslav's family helping your father leave Russia? I feel like I'm missing something here. What does this device do?"

They'd had close to a year apart. How easily she forgot there was so much he didn't know. So much she had to tell him in such a brief time. Some things could wait until later. She twisted the blue topaz ring on her finger.

"It doesn't matter." She'd soon be on a plane, and Alysa would help her keep hidden so Ivan couldn't find her. Perhaps in another year, they would both forget about this meeting. Nash had Gina to help him move on, and she'd dive back into another project to lose track of the days and hours since last seeing him.

"I shouldn't have gotten you involved in this. I'm sorry. You can go back to your baseball game with your family and forget I showed up on your door. Hopefully, it's not too late to keep you out of this."

"I'm not one of your father's employees anymore, Mila. You can't dismiss me." His voice had an edge to it, an underlying warning. She'd heard it in his voice once before, and he'd walked away then. It crushed her, and here she was, asking him to do it again.

He hadn't given her enough time to absorb the accusations he made against her father to react. He just left.

Not another word. Nothing.

But that was then, and this was now. At least she wouldn't be left questioning his feelings and sorting her own.

She glared at him. Her entire body strung tight as time slipped away from her—every second costing her the ability to escape and keep her livelihood secure.

She closed her eyes, gave in to the fact that his nearness brought her comfort. For both their sakes, she needed to push him away. The sight of him kissing Gina was coming back to the forefront of her mind.

"You don't have anyone else to turn to, do you?"

Truly, Nash was the only one.

"I have a friend, Alysa. I can stay with her until my father returns, and we handle the situation."

Perhaps after all this, her father would find her worthy of running the company.

She just had to stop Ivan from controlling their very livelihood.

———

"Police! Anyone here?"

Nash doubted he would get more answers from Milena.

"Up here. Be down in a minute."

Footsteps sounded on the stairs.

"We are not finished." Nash pointed at her.

Milena swept up some clothes and stuffed them in a bag. "Your *friend* is downstairs waiting for you."

Nash raked his hand through his hair.

An officer ducked his head in the bedroom. "In here."

Another one joined them. "Someone reported a break-in."

"I did." Nash raised his hand.

"Is this your place?" the first officer asked, a dark-skinned gentleman with a round face and some weight hanging over his belt.

"Mine." Milena bent down, picked up a blouse, and several other items.

"I'm Officer Brumel."

"Milena Borghese." Milena slung the bag strap over her shoulder. "As you can see, someone broke into my home and trashed the place. Mr. Dunford was kind enough to call you."

She glanced around on the floor.

Office Brumel followed her gaze. "Is there anything missing?"

"I'm not sure," Milena answered. She moved over near the closet. "Excuse me, officer, I lost my shoes on the way here, and I'd like to fetch another pair in my closet."

Office Brumel stepped out of the way.

"May I inquire how you lost your shoes?"

"Ask that one." She waved back to Nash.

He cleared his throat. "She was running. She thought someone was after her. We reported it earlier to Officer Gina Fullerton."

"And you are?"

"Nash Dunford."

"You're a friend of Ms. Borghese?"

He heard her make a noise from inside the closet and ignored it. She was the one who showed up asking him for help.

"You could say that."

Nash's phone buzzed, and his brother sent him an update on the game and asked how he was doing. He would have to wait to text him back.

"Do you have an idea of when the break-in could have happened?"

Milena returned, wearing a pair of black flats with a buckle on each side. He supposed for her, those were sensible shoes.

"I left the house around six-forty this morning. Usually, it's earlier, but my driver ran into traffic and was ten minutes late."

"So, the house has been empty since the time you left until now?"

"We got here twenty minutes before you did," Nash said.

"No pets?"

"No." She smiled sadly.

Nash had tried to get her another dog when her fluffy Pomeranian had passed away three months after he had been assigned to securing her part of the building. Her forlorn looks could torture a man's soul. Plus, a dog, an enormous dog, could have added extra security to keep her safe.

She hadn't wanted a big dog.

Nor had she wanted him, or she hadn't according to her father. His pride wouldn't let him approach her after she'd dismissed him in his attempt to warn her of the trouble her father had brewing.

But she believed her father was a victim just like her.

And she would. Because Mila Borghese looked at everyone and saw the good in them. She'd always been too trusting.

Until she hadn't.

Nash followed the officers and Milena downstairs.

Gina stood in the living room, with the other officer that came with Brumel.

"May I see your phone?" Milena asked, catching Nash off guard.

He handed it to her as Gina approached him. He stepped away, not paying attention to who Milena called, and stayed between the two women.

"There is no forced entry that we can find," Gina said.

Nash stuffed his hands in his pockets. He turned his head slightly to hear Milena's conversation, but she seemed to stare at his screen more than talk.

"The door was open when we got here," Nash said.

"She could have left it open. This seems odd, Nash. She shows up at your house. Claims her driver is dead, but there is no body. You bring her home, and the place is trashed, and the door left unlocked. Nothing is missing."

He got where Gina was going with this.

Nash held up his hand. "She paled when she came inside."

"Probably because you caught what a slob she is. What happened, the maid quit?"

He didn't like Gina's sarcastic tone.

"They cut the cushions. The mattress is flipped and shredded upstairs. Someone was looking for something. They could have found the key she keeps hidden."

"Or had a key," Gina shrugged.

He crossed his arms, irritated he had gotten trapped between these two women. The entire situation was making him uneasy. "Milena's the neatest person I've ever met. She also wouldn't have shredded her furniture or messed up her perfectly organized closet. I know her."

Gina placed her hands on her hips and glanced over at Milena, then back at him. "It's been a year. People change. She could be setting you up."

It had crossed his mind a few times.

Milena appeared relieved as she came toward him and held out his phone. "Thank you."

"I think we're done here." Officer Brumel approached them. "If you find anything missing, let us know. I'm glad you're safe."

Milena frowned.

Gina grinned as a flashy silver sports car pulled into the drive. She walked to the door.

A tall man, with long wavy black hair and sunglasses, got out of the car. He had on leather loafers and pressed slacks.

Milena froze.

"Who is that?" Nash asked.

Gina leaned into him. "I'm guessing that is Mr. Yaroslav."

"Her father's business associate," Nash said.

Gina pulled back, her eyes narrowed. "Her fiancé."

Milena backed deeper into her condo.

The man walking toward them frowned. His long, dark hair was pulled back in a ponytail, black as the goatee on his chin. Nash didn't like the way the guy's eyes narrowed on him.

"Where is Milena?"

Nash glanced behind him. She was gone. A muscle in his neck tightened.

"Where did she go now?" Gina threw up her hands.

"I'll find her." Nash headed through the living room to the kitchen. The back door stood open.

"Seriously?" he muttered, taking off in a jog into the center of the landscaped area behind the row of condominiums.

"Where is she?"

Nash turned. Ivan Yaroslav stood in the back door. "What have you done with Milena?"

"Me?" Nash pointed to his chest. "I don't know what you're talking about."

Ivan's eyes narrowed. "I know you."

"I doubt it." Nash would have recognized the face and the name.

"Are you a cop, then?"

"Do I look like a cop?"

Ivan's chin notched. "No. What business do you have here?"

"He's with me," Gina said from behind Yaroslav. "Nash works with me as a consultant on special cases."

Ivan nodded. "I see. Milena is probably confused and frightened. She could be in great danger. We must find her."

"She was just here," Gina said.

"You lost her already?"

"No. I mean. Yes." Gina scowled. "We found her. We had no reason to detain her in her own home."

"Incompetence." Ivan sniffed.

Nash could see the anger boiling beneath Gina's surface.

"Perhaps she stepped out for some air?"

"What are you doing just standing here?" Ivan glared at Gina.

"Whoa there, man. No crime, no reason to hold her.

You and your girlfriend are having a dispute that's not the police's problem," Nash said.

Ivan tugged on the end of his suit sleeves. "I recommend you stay out of this. It is an issue between myself and the authorities."

Nash held up his hands, whistled, and turned away.

"Find her." Ivan walked back through the house, calling out Milena's name at the top of the stairs.

"No one up there," an officer said.

Nash glanced over his shoulder, and Gina gave him a dirty look. She moved to catch up with Yaroslav.

Slowly, Nash surveyed their surroundings for one last time.

Where did she go?

5

Mila slipped inside the back of Nash's truck. She huddled between the seats, clutching her purse and pulling the jacket down over her. Holding her breath, she listened as several cars drove past and men shouted around the truck.

After what felt like forever, the front door of Nash's truck opened.

"If she calls or contacts you, promise you'll contact me first and let the police handle this," Gina said.

"She's in trouble."

"Is she?" Gina's voice sounded wistful. "You once told me she's high maintenance and not your style. Don't let her pull you back into her web. She made you lose your job. You were good at what you did. I'd hate to see you fall back after all the progress you've made."

"I've got this, Gina," Nash said.

The driver's door creaked open wider. Milena held her breath, waited. She squeezed her eyes shut, dreading the thought of them using their mouths for something other than talking. It was worse than Ivan finding her.

"We still on for tomorrow evening?" she asked, her voice a little more breathless.

Milena strained to hear. It was wrong, but she couldn't help herself.

"Wouldn't miss it," Nash said.

A moment later, the truck door shut, and she heard the engine start. Nash sat for a minute, checking his phone and taking the time to fasten his seat belt.

As the truck moved, Milena tried to relax. Nash's jacket made her sweat, and his spicy aftershave surrounded her, making it hard to breathe under the leather. A piece of the zipper scratched against her cheek.

The radio came on with a catchy tune, but Nash wasn't singing. The truck hit a bump, and Milena's knee let out. She yipped as it banged against the footboard.

"What the—?" The truck swerved, and Milena glanced at Nash's momentarily surprised face. His gaze went back to the road. "Mila?"

He practically growled at her and Mila gritted her teeth.

"Just keep driving, will you?" Her heart raced as she panicked that he would stop the truck and try to kick her out—or worse, scold her for rash behavior.

"What do you think I'm doing?" Nash muttered.

She pushed the coat from her and slid up in the back seat.

"Stay down."

Milena lay across the seat, forgetting about a seat belt. "You think someone is following us?"

"Don't you?"

Yeah, he had her there. Milena stayed down. She wouldn't put it past Ivan to follow Nash. Had Ivan recognized Nash?

Nash's arm muscles flexed, and she admired the strength in him. She missed those arms. Remembering the last time he wrapped them around her, her body flushed. Was it her, or was it getting hot in here?

"I'll take you to a secure location, but first, you need to spill. I mean it, Mila."

Hearing the tone of his voice, Mila took a deep breath. There was no use in getting him more agitated. "I told you."

"Oh yeah? You forgot to mention your engagement. Yaroslav? This better not be a love spat between the two of you while Daddy is out of town."

Mila narrowed her eyes. She bit the inside of her cheek before she spoke. Ivan would make the authorities think she was unstable and a danger to herself to get to her. No one would believe her if she took the stand against him.

"My father arranged it. It's not like I got asked." She gripped the side of the seat as the truck took a sharp turn. "Where are we headed?"

"Would you have told me?"

"What would it matter? You're the one who left and found a new *friend*." She hated the taste of those words as they spilled out.

"I am still your friend, Mila. Always." The truck slowed. Milena's heart pounded harder. They came almost to a stop when a shadow blocked the light from the window. She realized they'd pulled into a parking garage. He drove around several levels until he picked a spot on the third and parked.

"Why are you parking? They'll find us here. Yaroslav could have any of his men following us."

Nash put his arm across the seat and gazed back at her.

"We didn't get to finish our conversation." Slowly,

Milena sat up, her stomach tightening, twisting. She glanced around the parking garage. "Talk fast. It won't take long for them to figure out where we went or that I'm parked here."

Nash's expression softened, his gaze steady. Emotions twisted inside her. She wanted to believe he was the one. The guy who would keep his word. The one who could keep Ivan from stealing her father's company and protect her from his plans.

A dawning of understanding struck her speechless.

"Mila? I don't like that look."

"It's nothing. Sickness from nerves." She shook her head.

"I know that look, and you're not turning green," Nash said.

The sound of a car coming up on their level sent her pulse racing. "Someone is coming," she all but hissed through her teeth.

"It could be Yaroslav or one of the men with him when he arrived at your place," Nash agreed with her.

He had her where he wanted her. She stiffened, keeping low in case the vehicle came past them.

"My father arranged it."

"Makes sense. How long have you known?"

"What?" She sweated more.

"You and Yaroslav?"

"Jealous?" A girl could hope, couldn't she?

The car slowed, crept past. Nash pulled his keys from the truck and locked the steering wheel. "Not them, unless Yaroslav sends women with pouting kids in the back of their cars to check up on you.

Milena pressed her damp forehead to the warm vinyl on the seat. "My father told me a few days before you came to me with your theory I thought you knew. I thought that was why you'd said those things. Then you took off and didn't return."

"I guess your father didn't tell you he fired me."

"No. Nor did you." Maybe it was the smell of hot leather, or the spicy cologne Nash wore embedded in the surrounding air. Or the pressure building in the truck cab from the lack of air. She almost asked him to wind down the windows.

"Your betrothed wouldn't have been happy." Nash's voice coated with regret.

Sounds of a door slamming in the distance made her jump. "Can we go now?"

"You're free to get out of this truck anytime you want."

And in her gut, she knew he meant it. Whatever made her think she could trust him or that he cared made her ill.

"Can you crack the windows? It's stuffy in here."

"Get out, Milena." Nash opened his door, reached back, and opened the one behind him for her to get out.

"Leaving again, Nash?" She swallowed down the bile rising in her throat. Not again. Could their friendship have meant nothing to him? Did he believe her father fired him? *Oh, Father, what mess have you gotten me into?*

Nash got out of the truck, reached in, and yanked her out. "Miss me much? "

Milena caught the edge in his voice, the deepening lines of his forehead. She shoved away from him. He wouldn't put this on her. She wouldn't let him. Nash Dunford didn't get to be let off the hook that easily, not when his rejection had caused her such turmoil in the weeks and months after he walked away. Shocked and shattered, she had been the one to go through the motions, the engagement, and her father's sense of duty over family.

It had gotten all of them in this mess.

She grabbed her bag and pulled back her shoulders. At least for now, she was away from Ivan.

"Thank you, Nash." She owed him that.

Milena tucked away the disappointment and the expectations she allowed to seep from the place she kept her emotions locked. "I'm sorry you had to miss spending time with your family. I hope the Orioles won today. It was nice seeing you again."

His body tensed. His eyes narrowed, and, down a little way, someone slammed a car door shut. She tried not to flinch. In the past twelve hours, she'd grown jumpy.

"So that is it? You come asking for my help, and you dismiss me?"

It ratcheted her insides, tightening and tightening them until it became hard to breathe. She was wasting precious time. She could be on her way to the airport.

"It was a mistake to get you involved."

"To get me involved, or for catching you at your game?"

Shocked, she stepped back. "This isn't a game."

Nash's right brow lifted, but before she could say another word, a gunshot echoed through the parking garage. Glass shattered in the car window next to her.

"Get down!" Nash shoved her to the concrete. Voices shouted from down the row. Nash eased off her, peered around the truck, while Milena hugged the back tire of his truck.

The sound of a vehicle. People talking. Feet moving. Milena wanted to look, but Nash held her back, his hand firmly on her upper arm. His expression went from annoyed to dark. She shivered and said, "Some game, right?"

Another shot rang out, and the sound of it pinging off

metal sent Milena's nerves on edge. Forgetting about the tire, she leaned against Nash's back. "What do we do?"

"Get out of here." Nash moved, pulling Milena behind him. He opened the door to his truck, and she moved to get in.

"Not there." Nash stopped her.

Shouts got closer, and Nash gritted his teeth. Milena rose to peer over the bed of the truck. "Anton."

Nash yanked her back down, and she landed on her butt. He searched in his truck, ripping up the seats and shoving things out of the way. All the while, she listened, the drumming of her heart blocking all other sounds.

Then Nash grabbed her, tugged on her. "Stay down."

He pointed for her to slip around the front of the truck.

One by one, they ran and ducked behind vehicle after vehicle.

"There." Nash directed her attention to the door leading to the staircase out of the parking garage. They'd have to run across the open area to reach it.

"On three," Nash whispered.

Milena inhaled, trying to ease the pressure in her chest. She had suspected Ivan of many things, but sending Anton to kill her hadn't been one of them. Ivan stood to gain many things with her alive. Why would he want her dead?

She rose, every nerve of her body going on alert.

"Get down. I didn't say three," Nash said.

"They won't shoot me. Ivan needs me." Her legs trembling, she glanced and saw the top of Anton's bald head.

"Tell that to the guys with guns."

Milena glanced around and froze. A gun pointed in her direction. The man's eyes widened, his lips turned into a sneer. This wasn't Anton. The man held his gun just like the one who shot Benson. Cold filled her veins, and her muscles tightened up.

"You will come with us, Miss Borghese." The man's Russian accent was thick, or perhaps he'd spoken in his language. Either way, she would have understood him. Those evil eyes focused on her. His jaw was smooth-shaven, and while he wasn't wearing a scarf to cover it, she felt a sense of familiarity.

Out of the corner of her eye, she spotted Anton.

The man shouted something in Russian. In the next instant, he went down. Nash tackled the man, and they rolled across the wide area. Nash tried to disarm him.

"Get out of here!" Nash grunted. He had a hold of the man's hand with the gun and slammed it down on the concrete. Anton started running toward her.

Milena raced over to where Nash struggled, kicking the gun from the man's hand, and it went flying down between the cars. Nash punched the guy, and Milena jumped back.

"Go," Nash said.

She took off for the door, a shot hitting the glass and cracking it. Nash was right behind her, yanking it open and shoving her into the stairwell. A second later, Anton slammed against the door, and Nash held onto the bar to keep the other man from barging through.

6

Nash pulled on the door, and the other man pressed his face to the glass, growling at him. "I see they don't teach manners where you're from," Nash grunted. "It's not nice to shoot at a lady," he said.

Milena hesitated.

"Go!"

"I can't just leave you!"

Nash tightened his grip as the man on the other side of the door tried to jerk it open. The man pounded on the heavy metal between them. "Any time now, Mila."

She made a face, ill, desperate, then turned and raced down the stairs.

Nash had only seen the two of them. He'd knocked the other guy out cold, but Nash hadn't the time to find his gun. The one he kept under the seat in his truck. Thanks to Milena, the other guy's weapon had gone flying out of reach.

His arms strained to pull on the door and keep the other guy from getting in. Nash said something his mother would have slapped him for once Milena went out of sight. He could hear her footsteps pounding down the stairwell.

With no other options, Nash shoved instead of pulled, knocking the other man off balance. He took off down the stairs after Milena. He leaped several stairs at a time to the landing. He nearly pushed her down the last flight. A bullet whizzed by his arm, a hot slice through his skin, and hit the wall. He jerked to the left, hit the wall, and stumbled into Milena.

She ducked and screamed and hunched on the landing. He fell into her, both of them caught off balance, and rolled down the stairs to the next landing. Every bone in his body jarred, Nash pushed up, a sting in his arm, and his muscles screamed from the brunt of the fall. He grabbed her by the waist, lifting and pushing, the door at the bottom of the stairwell in sight.

"You okay?"

He didn't give her a chance to answer. Nash lifted and dragged her to the next set of stairs. "Go. Go. Go."

Down at the bottom of the stairs, Nash shoved the door open. Milena pushed through, and he slammed it just as the man came into view, running down the stairs. As the door shut, Nash pulled out a multi-tool from his back pocket and twisted the tiny screw in the door handle, locking the door between them.

Nash grabbed Milena by the hand, and they ran from the parking garage. Outside, he squinted as the late afternoon sun sent a glare over the traffic. They wouldn't have much time before rush hour. He slowed as they hit the sidewalk and saw more people. Scanning the traffic, the people, and the storefronts ahead, Nash caught Milena about to look over her shoulder. "Don't."

He shortened his stride, noticing the way she had to jog

to keep up with him He laced their fingers together. Up ahead, he spotted the light turning red. They were almost there.

There was no doubt in his mind this wasn't a game. He appreciated Gina looking out for him, her concern, and her friendship. He glanced over at Milena. Desperation and something she hadn't told him yet caused her to frown. He gave her hand a squeeze, the action sending a twitch of pain in his upper arm as it worked all those muscles. It reminded him they were alive. For now.

"Hungry?" he asked.

She gave him an incredulous look, and he laughed. It helped evaporate the tension. Her bag was about to slip off her shoulder. Nash caught it as he pushed her into the diner's cool interior.

"How can you think of your stomach at a time like this?"

The two men had shaken her. Her skin was pale and sweaty. Her palm trembled against his. He gave her the broadest smile, notched his chin up as he spotted Oliver at the counter. The big black man snorted at their approach. The supper crowd would soon trickle in.

"Come to rub it in, didn't you?"

It took him a moment to switch his gears from the events leading them here to the game Oliver was referring to.

"I take it the Twins won?"

Oliver growled. "Traitor."

Nash shrugged. "I just know the game. The loss hurt, man. Real bad."

Nash hit the center of his chest.

"I take it the lady isn't a fan?" Oliver put down a beefy

elbow on the counter and leaned forward. "What can I do you for?"

Nash sobered, tugging Milena closer. "Whatever you've got that's on the go."

"It's like that?" Oliver's gaze met his.

Nash nodded. The two of them had a deep under-standing ever since Nash saved Oliver's wife, Shirley, one night behind the café. She'd been about to get mugged when he stepped in and sent the teen ruffians sailing. No one messed with Momma Shirley. The woman might have balls of brass, but her punch wasn't as nearly as strong as the red sauce she served on her meatball hoagies.

"Favor for the lady."

Milena watched them. He kept hold of her, vowing he wouldn't let her go again. He'd made that mistake once. No one would scare him off a second time. He knew better, just as he knew before Big Ollie tilted his head. "In the back. Whatever you need."

Behind them, the door opened, and Nash slid his arm around Milena to give her strength. Maybe a little for him to pull her close. He would be the first to admit he'd been scared there for a minute in the stairway until he remem-bered the multi-tool he'd slipped in his pocket earlier when he was searching for his gun in the truck.

"You're the man." Nash slapped the man's hand, gave him a hard shake, and tugged Milena behind him.

Heat and the wicked smell of peppers and fish assaulted him. They raced through the room to the back door, where Nash swiped a set of keys from the hook.

"Oh, no, you don't!"

Nash put his hands up, turned, and grinned at Oliver's wife, Shirley, her hair in cornrows and a painted brow arched in his direction.

"You caught me, Momma." Everyone in this part of town called the middle-aged woman 'Momma' for she had a way of taking care of everyone she met.

"Take this and get out of here. I don't want you or your trouble in my kitchen again tonight." She held out a brown sack stained with grease on the front.

Nash grabbed the bag and handed it to Milena. Her eyes widened, and her lips parted. They didn't have the time for Nash to kiss the surprise out of them. He kissed Momma Shirley rather than appear the fool. One big loud smacking kiss on the side of her cheek. "You're the best!"

"You talk too loudly like that, and Big Ollie will serve you a knuckle sandwich." Shirley grinned, waving her hands. "Get. I've got food to prepare."

Out they went. Nash took a moment to glance down the back alley and across to the parking space where Oliver's aged Oldsmobile sat.

Nash waited for an *'I'm not riding in that,'* but Milena hugged the food bag and stared, wide-eyed, at their ride. He opened the car door and waited for her approach. "Would you prefer the back seat?"

Her cheeks tinted pink, the most color he'd seen since they stepped out of the kitchen.

"Everyone knows Big Ollie's got the best in town. Best woman. Best food, and best ride." Nash let his voice lower. "It'll keep you safe."

But who would keep her safe from him? Nash stepped closer. His front pressed to hers. Maybe he wanted to intimidate her a little. A warning of sorts to not get attached to him again. Because he most certainly wasn't getting attached to her.

She watched him with those guarded eyes. He could see

the heroism reflecting back at him. He wasn't anyone's hero. Especially not hers.

Nash reached around her and his entire body switched on alert, entirely too aware of the woman. Unable to resist, he tilted his head, his nose brushing alongside hers. A rich scent of sweetness a man couldn't ever get out of his memory filled him. Her lips were less than an inch away.

Milena's breath caught in her throat. She reached for him at the same time he reached for the car door. The click of it opening registered in their ears. Backing away a bit, Nash pulled the door the rest of the way open for her.

Her gaze landed on his.

If ever there were a time a man wanted to cut his own heart out, this was it. What kind of man was he to take advantage of a situation like this? He prayed he had the strength to do what was right by this woman. He had to keep her safe. No matter what.

The *'no matter what'* was the hardest part, knowing she would soon marry Yaroslav. Even if the guy had sent men to kill her. Not her. Him. Yaroslav got Milena. Nash had always only been an accessory.

"You need to get in." He clenched his jaw, pulled himself back into protection mode. He made the mistake of allowing things between them to get personal in the past. For both their sakes, they couldn't afford for it to happen again.

It took an extra-long moment before Milena nodded, tucking herself into the front passenger seat.

The adrenaline rush from the parking garage must have tapped out both their abilities to think clearly. Or maybe it'd been the way she'd looked at him, hopeful, that told him she hadn't closed off that part of her either.

He'd just have to see about that.

"You can drop me off at the airport," Milena said, slumped in the seat, peering out the side of her window.

Nash maneuvered them through five o'clock traffic, which was more like five thirty, but it made his teeth grind. It would take a good twenty to thirty minutes without the extra traffic to get her to her destination. Except the airport was south, and Nash headed north. They'd stick to the plan he formed in his head

"Why the airport?"

"I have a friend I can go visit until my father gets back to handle the situation."

He didn't like the listlessness in her voice. It tightened his vocals, and he rubbed his itchy hand against the steering wheel. Big Ollie's Oldsmobile was pimped, the steering wheel wrapped in crushed velvet against his sweaty palm. The entire thing was purple, like a box of Fruity Pebbles. Even the seat covers had specks of color across the black. But it smelled of grease and smoke and something fishy.

Milena's bag sat between her legs and the food on her lap. He counted to ten, sped up, and moved into another lane to get them closer to getting out of town. It didn't distract him from wanting to reach over and push the hair away from her cheek. He considered taking her hand in his again. He'd rather have his fingers entwined with hers then over the top of a fuzzy steering wheel.

"And what is the situation?" Nash slowed down, put on his turn signal, as they came to a halt thanks to a red light ahead. He glanced around, no signs of Tweedledee and Tweedledum. He'd tagged them both in his head to keep track of them. He kept a lookout for Yaroslav's car or the one that pulled in front of his house and the man looking for Milena. The same man, he acknowledged, that he'd trapped in the stairwell.

"Who was the guy in the stairwell? You knew him."

She'd said his name. What had it been?

Milena looked at him, her eyes heavy as her mind replayed the event. Nash watched for the light to change. He couldn't allow her to suck him back in with those gorgeous eyes of hers.

"Anton." She leaned back further in her seat. Sweeping that piece of hair from her cheek, she looked out ahead with him. "He took over as head of security for my father at Ivan's recommendation after you left."

"He got rid of me to infiltrate with his own people."

"It would seem."

He heard her stomach growl and said nothing. He knew it would embarrass her to point it out. He tried to think of the best place to take her and hide for the night while they tried to straighten this out. He should listen to Gina, take her to the police station, and let them handle this, but his gut told him she wouldn't be safe.

He pulled out his phone, handed it over to Milena. "Text Bryon. Tell him, 'Playing it safe.'"

"I don't know the code for your phone."

She probably knew that and everything else he had stored on his phone. Her father didn't give her enough credit. Milena Borghese was as brilliant as she was beautiful. It had been hard to keep their relationship strictly professional when he found her attractive. Even harder, when he spent late nights watching her clean up and troubleshoot to help the engineers who created some of the company's highly-sought-after digital advancements.

It had given him time to do some research of his own.

The light turned green, and Nash stuck with the traffic,

staying in the middle lane to keep them from being spotted. Because driving a purple Oldsmobile blended in well with the other cars. At least it had muscle and style compared to the hybrid cars dashing around them.

"It's your house number." It's how he remembered it. Couldn't bring himself to change it when he left.

She twisted her lips but said nothing. A moment later, she handed it back to him.

"You should call your father, maybe your friend."

Maybe the police, Nash thought, then changed his mind. Gina seemed to think Ivan and Milena were having a domestic spat. Men with guns didn't get involved with a lover's quarrel. He should ask if Ivan had to deal with any other Russian groups. For all he knew, Ivan and his associates could be terrorists or working for the mob.

She opened her mouth to speak, then closed it.

He kept his eyes on the road, mostly. Frequently, he glanced at her, the back mirror, the side mirror. So far, so good.

"Do you need me to pull up directions?" she asked.

"I know where I'm going." He hoped he did.

As he drove, he listened with the radio turned off. She wiggled in her seat, fished down in her shirt, and pulled out what appeared to be a fob. The little black device was no bigger than his thumb.

"What are you doing?"

She connected it to his phone. A light went from red to green. "I'm making a call of sorts."

She held the phone over their supper. "You did say I should make a call."

"Is that a tracking device?"

She grinned. "Not really. It's more of a listening device."

He'd gotten them out of the east harbor and headed to Jonestown.

His phone vibrated in her hand.

"Bryon asked if you've struck out yet."

Nash contemplated his response. Bryon would want to help him, and he couldn't pull his baby brother into something he himself didn't quite understand.

"Should I answer him?"

Nash shook his head. "I'll take care of it later. We're almost there."

"To the airport," she insisted.

Then his phone rang, and her hand trembled. "It's working."

Before he could ask, she swiped her finger and put another to her lips until he noticed that she wanted him to remain silent. With the speakerphone activated, they listened as two voices held a conversation.

"We lost them in the parking garage."

"You were to tail them, not lose them!"

Yaroslav.

"We had an opportunity. I take it." The man's English awkward.

"Obviously not," Yaroslav said.

"We will find her."

"Where is Anton? Why isn't he calling me?"

"He is checking into another possibility."

"There is only one other place she'd go," Yaroslav said. "Take Malcolm and Viktor to the airport. If I know Milena, she'll be on the first plane after her father. We need to intercept her before the cops do any more snooping."

"Yes, sir."

The phone clicked.

Milena hugged the phone and the sack of food.

"It's a good thing we are not headed to the airport."

Quietly, she turned her head to stare out the side window. He watched her back, the rise and fall as she took deep breaths. "I don't know any other place to go."

"I do."

7

They parked in front of an apartment building on Granby. Milena chewed on her lip. This had gotten way out of hand. Her first thought was to call her father, but she couldn't leave traces on Nash's phone. Her father had been clear about contacting him, secretive, and she couldn't blame him.

Maybe she should go to the police, but they'd hand her over to Ivan.

Nash reached between her legs for her bag. Sharply, she glanced over at him. He reached instead for the food. "Okay, there?"

She'd gotten jumpier with each passing minute.

"Where are we?"

"Somewhere safe. Come on."

Inside the building, Nash let them into an apartment on the second floor. Down the hall, beatbox music drifted, and voices rang out. Nash ushered her into the apartment.

"Sean is out of town. He asked me to check in on the place."

"For how long?"

She relaxed a little since they'd gotten out of the car. According to the communication device, at the time of the call, Ivan was back at his place.

"Until he gets back."

She put her hand on her hip.

"Chill, Mila. Your boyfriend isn't going to find us here if that's what you're worried about."

"What are we doing here?"

Nash put the bag down on the bar separating the kitchen from the living area. He pulled out a stool. "Hungry?"

He walked around into the kitchen, helped himself to a can of soda, and grabbed a second. "Still the no-caffeine-before-bed type?"

"I see you haven't lost that chip on your shoulder."

He slid one can of soda across the counter toward her. He leaned by the sink, peered out the window.

"What?"

She leaned forward, and he grinned at her. "I'll check the other rooms and make sure the windows are secure. Then we'll eat."

He didn't give her the chance to protest. She dropped her bag at her feet. She moved over to the door. Nash had locked it. Outside, the inaudible hum of the music breached the walls. Photographs of a man rock climbing caught her attention. Another picture of that same man in a group and another with him and a woman.

Whoever this guy was, he liked the outdoors. Would he appreciate two people hanging out in this place without him home?

"We're good. You good?"

The warmth of his nearness hit her first.

His fingers wrapped around her upper arms.

She wanted more than anything to lean back against him. "Don't you need to call your brother or something?"

"I'll check in with him after we eat. It would be a shame to let Momma Shirley's gift go to waste."

"It's probably cold," she said.

"I've got you covered."

That was what she feared.

Nash stepped away. She turned and watched him get out the food, heat it in the microwave.

"This is your plan? We come here and eat?"

The truth was, she was starved. She'd had a protein bar heading out to the office and three cups of decaf latte all day.

Outside, the sky had turned an ominous gray. Daylight Saving Time hadn't done them any favors. She sank onto a stool.

"We can't go back to my place or yours." Nash set a plate with a meatball hoagie and fries in front of her. He tapped on the soda closest to her. "No caffeine."

"You remembered?" Caffeine gave her headaches.

Nash put another plate down, stood on the other side of the counter. "I remember everything about you, Mila." His eyes and his voice made her stomach quiver. He'd remembered, but he made the choice to stay away.

"You're still wearing the necklace I gave you." His gaze fell to the silver cross hanging close to her heart.

She reached and tucked it back beneath her shirt, flustered and a little embarrassed that he saw it. "Yeah, well. Someone once reminded me there is a greater good at work."

It was the night he'd accused her father. The night he asked her to trust him. Believe him. Have faith.

She picked up a fry. "Find any ketchup in there when you were grabbing drinks?"

Nash pulled a half-empty bottle of ketchup and a jar of mayonnaise out. "There's only one bedroom. You can take the bed tonight. I'll sleep out here on the couch."

"Who says I'm staying here tonight?" She squirted ketchup, and he opened the jar of mayonnaise. A disgusting habit, but she watched him dip his fries in it anyway.

"I'll drive you to another airport in the morning if that's what you want. We can go to Dulles as long as they're not on our tail. But, Mila, I think I deserve to know what is going on. I meant it in the parking garage. What's up with Ivan and those guys back at the parking garage? If I didn't know better, I'd say they were trying to kill you."

She bit into her fry, chewed it slowly, and tried swallowing. She choked, and Nash reached over to pound on her back. Tears streaming down her face, she shook her head, catching her breath.

"The man in the parking garage. The one with Anton. I saw him. I think he's the one who shot Benson."

Nash sat back down. He wrapped his hand around his drink. "You think?"

"I'm not sure. I didn't see his face that well. But back in the parking garage, I think it was him."

"But not the other guy."

"No." She wiped her mouth, not wanting to cough again.

"They were both at my house. Looking for you."

She took a big gulp of her clear fizzing soda.

"Ivan must have had me followed. I should have been more careful. It was very stupid of me."

"No." Nash held a fry in his hand. His jaw tightened,

and those critical eyes of his eased. "I'm glad you came to me, Mila. I've missed you."

She smirked, tucking back a piece of hair falling forward against her cheek. "You say that now, but when this is over, you'll be glad I'm gone again."

He grimaced and stuck a fry in his mouth and chewed while he talked. "And will you be glad to be free of Ivan?"

She tore off a piece of her sandwich and stared down at the food. Her stomach was empty, unlike all the emotions spreading through her. She bit her lip, trying to compartmentalize them and hold them at bay. She promised she wouldn't become one of those females who fell apart after the adrenaline wore off.

"You want to know what is going on? I'll tell you." She tossed down the piece of bun. "My father left town a few weeks ago. My mother has been in a tizzy in his absence. She keeps questioning me about his whereabouts as if he told me." She picked up the piece of bun again, thought to stuff her face to keep from saying more, then waved it as she spoke. "I've suspected someone has been leaking information to our competitor. I've tried speaking with my father about it, but he doesn't seem to want to listen to me beyond new tech ideas. He assigned the Telek project to me."

"You're a smart woman."

She ignored his flattering comment. "Boyko Technology has been creating devices similar to ours. Six months ago, we kept our update to our window screen technology quiet, a surprise release, but then they announced the same upgrade a few days before ours was scheduled to launch."

"That's not too far after they forced me to resign."

Resign? She figured he left. Her father told her he'd quit. Too many things were happening at the same time. Too much information to process at once. It stuck in her chest, the way he looked at her. Not once had Ivan ever looked at her with anything more than anticipation and greed in his eyes.

Milena toyed with a fry. "Ivan. He came when you left."

"Your father hired him?"

"I wish it were that simple. If he were any other employee, I could have fired him. And with proof, I could have had him arrested. Simple."

"But not simple," Nash said.

"My father has no sons. In the beginning days of coming to America, he made a promise to the man who helped him fund his and my mother's travels that landed them in New York. My father had no choice. The KGB was after him. A few months after I turned school age, they moved here—better business, he said. Then, a few months before you left, he went to Ukraine, and Ivan appeared."

"I don't follow," Nash said.

"Ivan is the son of the man who helped my father out of Russia."

"And you marrying him was part of the deal."

"Yesss," she said through her teeth, slowly.

"And Boyko?"

"I think Ivan is selling them company trade secrets. I had my suspicions at first. Then you came to me, and I knew you were right about what was happening, but it couldn't have been my father. At first, I thought it was one of our people in our tech lab, and if it was, they were giving Ivan the information. I wasn't sure until he asked me for the password to Father's computer. He's too smart to sell out a company he's about to inherit through marriage. There has to be something else." She wished she knew.

"Whatever the reason, he is willing to kill for it."

Not Ivan. He wouldn't dirty his hands with the deed. He sent Anton to do it for him, but it hadn't been Anton who killed Benson. She hadn't been able to see his face, but the more she thought about it—she had time to think about it—the more certain she was that it was the guy in the parking garage.

"They might not have found a body, but I saw what I saw." Her chest rattled with grief for a man who attacked her.

"Dead men don't drive off in their cars, sweetheart."

"No, but the guy who did it could have."

"I think the first thing we need to do is find out for sure. In the morning, we'll go back to the place and look for ourselves."

No. She wouldn't go back there. Milena needed to get to an airport and get as far from here as possible. Although doubt seeped into her, causing her to wonder if she was making the wisest decision. No more people need to get involved. She couldn't risk anyone getting hurt, or worse, killed.

"The police were there. They didn't find anyone."

"You'd recognize the car?" Nash asked.

"Of course," she said.

Part of her was certain. Another part of her was trying to recollect flashbacks of what happened. The black Mercedes belonged to Borghese. It had happened so fast. Benson demanded the files. His desperation. His eyes. Lifeless.

Yes. She had seen it. It shook her to the core.

She hadn't been wearing her faith around her neck, or her heart on the end of her sleeve when it happened. But she had them on now, with Nash shoveling fries in his mouth and chewing as if they were having a normal conversation.

"The thing that Ivan is after?"

Neither one of them was safe with it.

"He won't get it. My father's company is about to go under if we lose any more of our technologies to Boyko. Plus, all those toy devices for retail are a cover for our government contracts. We can't lose them."

They'd all but lost this one government contract. Ivan wouldn't know about them. Her father would have taken precautions not to allow Ivan in on the dealings. Not yet. He wasn't family. And her father insisted he handle them. His office assistant, Diane, didn't touch them.

Milena did.

It was the one thing her father trusted her with in the company.

Or had he? Ivan would soon become part of the family with their marriage. Had her father shared this part of their business with him? How else would he know about the plans?

"That thing you used to tap into my phone to listen to his call. That was it?"

She blinked, her food forgotten. "A prototype. Yes."

"Are there any more?"

Milena shook her head. "No. I have the only one. My father and I were working on it together." He'd come to her after many attempts had failed. By sheer luck, or maybe a little divine intervention, she found a workaround to her father's original idea, and together they'd made it better.

For the first time, her father had treated her as an equal. Like father, like daughter, the digital engineering genes had passed from one to the other.

Where had divine intervention gone when she'd been

born a female and disappointed her father's yearning for a son?

She waited for the shock to register on Nash's face. Any moment, but none came. She hoped one day her father would have the same faith in her that Nash once had.

"What else does it do?" Curiosity brimmed over in his voice.

Digital gadgets and technology had a way of turning men into hungry boys.

"I can track where the device is at the time of the call. It is tapping into its records, but the storage to hold data is limited and must be downloaded onto another device to save long term."

"Sounds more like a spy gadget than selling retail."

Somehow, she could hear him saying that long before the words came out of his mouth.

"Why do you think Boyko wants it? This device is top secret. The contract for it far exceeds anything my father and I have ever created. It's worth millions. Which is why we can't afford to lose the contract on it."

Her father had started Borghese Technology as a cover for the work he did for the government. "After leaving Russia, my father made a deal with the American Embassy, and for the past two-and-a-half decades, he ensured government agencies were the first to bid on his technological advancements."

Nash's eyes widened. His lips went into a grim line.

"My father wouldn't want our technologies in the hands of the ones who forced him to leave his homeland. I think it had to do with one of his creations that caused him to leave in the first place."

"Where is your father?"

"I don't know. He wouldn't tell me where he was going.

All he said to Diane was that he'd be out of town for a couple of weeks. He didn't even tell my mother."

"Coward," Nash grunted.

"You misjudge him." Would they ever move past this? She wanted to believe they would, but right now, she had no clue where to go from here. No airport. No father.

Ivan wouldn't give up.

Neither would Nash.

"I call it as I see it." Nash crossed his arms.

"And I think I need to call it a night." She moved past him, paused for a moment. "We are staying here tonight, correct?"

"The bedroom is all yours." He waved in the door's direction. "In the morning, we'll go to the police."

"You mean Gina?"

"Yeah, you got a problem with that?"

"No." She shrugged. "Why would I?"

The truth was, she'd rather face Ivan than Nash's woman friend.

Have a little faith, Milena.

8

They'd had far too much going on for one day.

At least they were both alive.

Milo Borghese would have to answer to Nash later as to why the man would run off into hiding and leave his only daughter to defend the company secrets. There was more here. It lurked in the back of his mind and whispered in the dark to him. Maybe it was something Milena hadn't said to him. Maybe it was something she didn't know and couldn't tell him. What piece here was he missing? If anything at all.

Or maybe it was just Milena filling his mind and making his brain unable to quiet for him to sleep.

Nash lay in the darkness. With the exception of the thump and boom from the neighbors, the apartment building had quieted down close to midnight. He heard Milena shower just after nine. Did she sleep as comfortably in another man's bed as he did out on the couch?

He should have made an excuse to sleep in the same room with her. He could have shared the big king-sized bed Sean had in there. He wouldn't have touched her, but he needed to see her and be near her, and he vowed to keep her safe. Secret tech gadgets and family debts could wait.

His mind couldn't let go of trying to figure out Yaroslav. Why would a guy like Ivan Yaroslav, who would inherit the company, be selling its secrets to another?

He stared at the ceiling. Earlier, he called Bryon. A dark, unmarked car stayed parked outside Nash's place. He'd been wise to come here. If he were a betting man, he'd bet they were watching Milena's place, too.

Big Ollie would want his car back in the morning. Maybe he could talk Shirley into brunch, but that would be too late. Milena had hardly eaten.

This whole situation wasn't good.

God, he prayed, *just let me get her out of this safe, okay?*

Gina sent him a text. She asked him if everything was all right. He didn't tell her if he'd found Milena or not. At some point, the chase needed to stop for them long enough to take a breath. A big long deep breath. He figured if he stayed away, the ache in his chest would heal. Only now it returned twofold and reminded him what a fool he'd been in trying to deny it.

He promised to always be her friend.

Was it this Yaroslav that made him want to go back on his promise?

How could he think to stay friends with a woman whose lips tormented him by chewing on a fry? Her eyes alone could drown a man in his yearnings. Yaroslav was after her money. Nash had been after her heart.

Getting attached to your client was rule number one of 'no-no's' in his business.

Quickly Milena had fascinated him. They'd become friends.

He'd fallen too deep in the love department, and it

failed him. He'd failed her. She hadn't been impressed when he dug into her father's business practices.

And there it was. The little light that clicked on.

Except before he could grasp it, the sound of jiggling at the door caused him to focus on the noise. He lay still as the front door of the apartment opened, caught on the chain. A soft sound, a curse, muffled behind the steel.

Nash waited. He tried to relax on the couch to keep his advantage.

A moment later, the chain snapped in two.

The intruder stepped inside. The lights remained off.

Something heavy hit the floor.

Nash's every nerve went on alert. Reaching under a cushion, he pulled out the chef's knife he had found in the kitchen. Glad he kept something handy. Angry his gun had gone missing from his truck.

Feet scuffed across the carpet. Closer.

Nash breathed in, held it, waited. He sprang as the black shadow moved beside the couch, grabbing the intruder and slamming them down on the coffee table. Glass shattered, and the sound of it splintered in the room.

A string of words followed, and Nash got thrown off by the intruder. Taken by surprise, he rolled on the carpet.

A moment later, the door in the hall opened. "Nash?"

"Get back inside," he grunted, getting to his knees and lunging at the man pulling up from the smashed coffee table.

"Nash? What the—"

He froze, and the light switched on. Milena stood in a T-shirt, showing her shapely legs. Like a deer caught in headlights, Nash stared and blinked. Then a hand reached for him. Nash took it and twisted it behind the intruder.

"Seriously?" the man called out.

Milena sucked in her breath.

Nash glanced down. "Sean?"

"We gonna do this? Really? In my house?"

Nash let him go. "Sorry. I thought you were someone else."

He got to his feet, offered Sean his hand. The shorter man glared at him. Getting to his feet on his own, Sean said, "Don't you got a place of your own to crash in? What are you doing, bringing a woman here?"

"They have both our places under surveillance," Nash said.

Sean cupped the back of his neck, his gaze going to Milena. "You in some kind of trouble?"

It sobered him. Sean's muscles relaxed and he stepped out of the mess that once had been his coffee table. "Gina know about this?"

What was it with all his friends thinking there was more between him and Gina?

"Yeah. We're planning to go to the police station in the morning to hash things out. We just need a safe place for the night. Sorry about your coffee table."

Sean put his hands on his hips. He hadn't taken his eyes off Milena. Color flushed in her cheeks. Nash didn't like the way Sean drank her in under the low lights of the lamp she'd switched on.

"I thought maybe some squatter, and I forgot to lock the sliding door." He tugged at his shirt, letting little pieces of glass trickle to the floor

Milena stayed on the other side of the couch. "You're the man in the photos on the wall."

"Sean Koval. This is my place."

"You're back early." Nash sank on the couch. "I didn't think you were coming home until Thursday."

Sean flicked more glass from his cargo pants. "Today is Thursday. Rough week?"

Rough twenty-four hours. Nash's gaze met Milena's. "Sean, this is Milena."

She tugged on her shirt, keeping it down at mid-thigh.

"I've heard that name." Sean stepped through the glass and around the couch.

Nash stood, his breath caught, and his muscles tensed. He had no reason to take the man down again. Except for the way he grinned at Milena.

Nash squeezed his eyes shut. He couldn't look at her like that. He lost that chance, or had he?

"I'll just grab my things and get out of your way," he heard Milena say.

"You're fine," Sean said.

Nash opened his eyes. Narrowed them on his friend. *Fine* indeed.

"I'll just go finish getting dressed. We should clean up the glass before anyone gets hurt."

Sean rolled back a shoulder and winced. "There's still a few hours until it's officially morning. We can leave it until later."

"I'll take care of it. My mess." Nash walked out around the couch. "Go back to bed. It's going to be a long day again tomorrow—today."

She gave a weak smile, one that didn't quite reach her eyes. "I wasn't sleeping. You'll wish to have your bed back. I'll get my things."

And a pair of pants, but Nash wouldn't tell her out loud he liked the view. He'd seen those legs in a skirt and should have shut down his brain before it recalled any more things he liked about her.

"I slept on the flight. You get some rest. Nash can clean up while I make the coffee."

She caught her bottom lip between her teeth. Nash walked over to her, leaned close. "You're tired, Mila. Lay down for a few more hours. We'll get through this together." He cupped her cheek, tempted to refresh his memory of pressing his lips to hers.

He heard Sean's foot crunch on the glass on the carpet and cleared the fog in his brain. They weren't alone.

And this wasn't the time to try to rekindle what they once had.

It was too dangerous. For them both.

He kissed her cheek.

She let out a lengthy breath.

"Sean's a good buddy of mine."

"Like Gina?"

"He's an adventure blogger. We're all in the same life circle at church. We meet every Thursday for lunch."

It must have been the loss of the adrenaline from earlier that made him feel the need to explain it to her.

"Thank you."

For what? For explaining something he shouldn't have explained.

She kissed him, a warm impression on his cheek that would last forever.

———

"So this is your thing now? Rescuing damsels in distress? I thought you ditched the security gig for fixing roofs." Sean kept his voice low while he pulled out the coffee pot, turned on the faucet, and filled it with water.

"I take it that it got too hot in the desert for you?"

"I hardly call Utah a desert. Now Vegas, I'll hike out in Red Rock any day. There's a sight to behold out there." Sean winked. He poured the grounds into the filter and closed it. "You're avoiding the question. She's the one you told me about, isn't she?"

"Yeah, she is." Nash sat on the stool she'd sat at hours ago while they ate one of Momma Shirley's specials. After Borghese let him go, he went through an awful period. Gina, Sean, and Oliver had helped pull him out of the dark. He told them about Milena, and at the time, he wouldn't have been any good for her. Not when he had been thinking more with his emotions than his head. What had he been thinking?

He hadn't. He should have kept looking into Borghese to prove his facts were right. He let losing his job, and Milena's silence, wound his pride. It took him months to pull out of the black mood and the ditch he dug before Bryon came to Baltimore, and his kid brother gave him a swift kick of reality. It hadn't been like him.

No one in the state would hire him for a security detail or even in private protection. He landed a job on a construction crew thanks to Bryon giving him a good word.

"I thought you said she wanted nothing to do you with you."

"No. I said her father let me go and warned me not to come near his daughter again."

Milena's father had made it more than difficult for him.

Sean leaned back against the counter. "She came to you?"

That had been his first mistake. He should have gone to her months ago. Bryon had convinced him to steer clear of getting entangled any further. He lost his job. Why hadn't Milena known?

Nash's stomach rumbled and not from the want of food.

"Obviously, she doesn't feel the same way," Sean said.

Nash spent too many hours rolling it around in his head when he should have let it rest.

"She doesn't know." And that stuck in his craw. Nash had good instincts when it came to people. Milo Borghese could lie to his daughter, but Nash knew that Milo Borghese wasn't the type of man to abandon his daughter. He might have run once before when things got tough, but why would he leave Milena to deal with Yaroslav?

"This is going back to the stuff you said you found out about her father? What is he? Russian mobster or something?"

The seriousness of his tone struck Nash if not for the twinkle in Sean's eye under the bright kitchen lights. He chuckled. Milo Borghese was anything but a mobster. A spy? No, the man might wear a suit, but in Nash's time at Borghese Technology he'd seen Mr. Borghese working with the technicians more than sitting behind his desk.

He was hiding something from his daughter.

But what?

And where did Yaroslav fall into this? Other than an arranged marriage.

"I can see the wheels turning. You're starting to smoke out the ears, man. What gives?" Sean asked.

"Milena said her father went out of town. She has no way to contact him."

"Odd." Sean grabbed two mugs from the shelf above the sink. "You think he went out of town or someone arranged it?"

That's what he liked about Sean. He might prefer hiking the desert and writing about the latest in outdoor gear and travel spots, but the guy always suspected the worst. Not that Nash could blame him after the incident that took Sean's wife from him. That kind of thing scarred a man for life.

"It wouldn't surprise me. Milena thinks Yaroslav is selling the company trade secrets to Boyko."

"Borghese out of the picture, Yaroslav would have access," Sean pointed out.

Nash tapped his fingers on the counter. "He would anyway. Once he marries Milena, he'd have a hold on the company."

"Say what now?" Sean paused mid-reach for the coffee pot.

Nash put his elbow on the counter, ran his hand through his hair, and sighed. "Yeah. That."

Sean nodded thoughtfully. He poured the coffee and shared his thoughts out loud. "So, Borghese knew you had a thing for his daughter. He made sure you weren't an obstacle for hooking his baby girl up with Yaroslav. And Yaroslav must be in trouble if he's selling out a company he is one day going to have control over. If not this thing he's after, there will be another."

"According to Milena, the company is going under. They're losing their edge in the market with their designs leaking to their competitor. And Borghese isn't just making simple communication devices. He's been supplying the tech to the government."

Sean slid a cup of joe in Nash's direction. The smell alone sent his senses on alert. Sean made a black and steep brew that could keep a man awake for days.

"This is heavy. You sure you want to get further involved? Maybe you should take this to Gina. Let the police handle it."

"I tried." Inhaling the coffee helped him think more of the task at hand and less and less of what being involved with Milena could do to his heart. He'd gone about things all wrong the last time.

In less than twenty-four hours, she'd turned his life upside down. He'd never said he loved her. What would she have thought about that?

First, he needed to keep her safe from Yaroslav.

"Yaroslav went to the police. He made them think this was a domestic dispute. Someone trashed Milena's place. They followed her to my place. Two guys in suits tried to take us out, or take Milena, in the parking garage near Momma Shirley's."

Sean whistled low. "I can't say I want to be in your shoes. You told Gina?"

"We're headed there this morning to report what happened yesterday and tell them what is going on."

"Good luck with that." Sean sipped his coffee, made a face. Yeah, his coffee wasn't the best tasting, but it worked. "I take it you won't be meeting for lunch today?"

Their weekly circle lunch. Nash looked forward to the fellowship and the food.

He heard the door, and Milena stood with her bag over her shoulder. She'd pulled her hair back into a ponytail. She appeared so much different in jeans and a long-sleeve blouse than her usual slacks or skirts. She wore flat Mary Janes, and she'd gone without makeup. Even at four in the morning, she put on a mask over the terror going on inside her.

She could cover up the dark circles under her eyes. However, she couldn't cover up the uncertainty in her gaze.

"I thought I told you to get some more rest." It came out gruff and more commanding than necessary.

She drew back her shoulders. "You don't get to tell me what to do."

Nash got off his stool. "If I'm keeping you safe, then I get to have a say in keeping you in the best condition to stay alive."

Sean pulled out the coffee pot. "Coffee?"

"No, thank you," she said.

Nash explained. "Decaf only."

"That's too bad." Sean put the pot away. "Mind if I finish this?"

"Of course not." She moved closer. "Thank you for allowing me your room. I am sorry again about intruding."

"Don't be." Sean got a serious look in his eye and said, "I haven't had a woman sleep in my bed for almost two years. The pleasure was mine."

Milena's cheeks flamed. Her lips parted.

"I see you didn't leave your charm behind in the desert." Nash gritted his teeth, kept his hands around the warm cup of joe.

Milena recovered, only a tinge of pink left on her cheeks. She pointed to the photographs. "Not even that one?"

Sean stared at the photo she referenced. The one with Sean and his wife, Megan. His smile was distant and shook his head. "Someday, we'll be in a place where I'll lie down beside her again."

He turned and tossed the rest of his coffee in the sink. "We'd better get this mess of yours cleaned up."

9

For the past four hours, Milena had experienced a whirlwind of emotions. She stood in the small kitchen area of
Sean's apartment, watching the two men clean up the
broken glass and toss the shattered frame of the coffee table
out on a balcony.

Several times, she caught Nash's gaze on her. He had
this way of looking at her that said everything would be
okay. He made her feel safe.

He made her feel loved.

And she'd missed that. Missed him.

How could she have been such a fool and not come to
him sooner?

Nash's phone rang, not the usual ring, but the one she
chose for when Ivan's phone received a call.

"Yaroslav." They said it together, almost in unison.

"Answer, but don't say a word." They needed to listen.

"Borghese." Ivan's voice with his rich accent filled the
phone.

Milena stiffened. For a moment, she thought he would address her, and then she realized he spoke to another.

"What are you doing, Ivan?"

Milena covered her mouth. That voice. It was a woman. No. It was her mother. Her gaze flew to Nash. She used her other hand to cover her heart. Be still, she chided. Her mother never liked Ivan. She agreed with the arranged marriage. After all, her parents' marriage had been arranged.

"I'm protecting what is yours, as you asked."

"You're being sloppy. Stop it. If Milena finds out what you are doing, she will not understand. She will not want to marry you."

"And what are you doing?" Nash murmured, his eyes narrowed. He held the phone between the three of them.

Milena gave him a sharp look. She needed to hear over the loud thundering of her blood pumping in her ears.

"As if she has a choice. I have done everything you have asked me to do, madam. Milena has been promised to me since we were children. If you back out on our deal, my father will demand blood payment. Are you willing to sacrifice your husband, then?"

A sharp intake of breath. Hers or her mothers, Milena couldn't be certain.

"You will leave Milo out of this. Understand?"

"You were wrong about the files," Ivan said calmly.

"The fob?"

"I believe Milena has it."

A pause, and then her mother said, "How? Milo assigned her to another project. I know this because I asked him to keep my daughter out of this."

Milena bit the inside of her cheek to keep from screaming. Not that they would hear her. Nash's free hand went to her arm. Squeezed gently.

"She caught me in Milo's office. I asked her for it."

"Stupid," her mother said. "Milena is not some meek housewife. She is smart. Very smart."

"Cunning. Like her mother. Do not worry. She is hiding from me, but I will find her. I suggest we move up the wedding date. The sooner she understands her place, the less complicated our future will become."

Her mother made a noise. One Milena recognized when her mother got upset or angry. She wouldn't want to be in the same room as the woman at this moment. Her mother tended to break things. Where was Mother's stress ball when she needed it?

The phone crackled.

Ivan said, "Is that a yes?"

"Make sure the client gets what he wants before the deadline. I will get a hold of Milena and the priest. Do this, and I will see she stands in the front of the church. You will have my blessing."

She had never heard her mother's voice so strained.

Ivan laughed. "Today. For I shall conclude this business on time."

"Impossible. We'll set the date for Saturday. Two weeks from now. Milena deserves more than a Vegas wedding. I shall get Milo and arrange for everything. Don't screw this up."

"A week," Ivan said.

"Two. I have to book the church."

"Fine. Two weeks, no later."

"Good. I have to call my daughter."

"She tossed her phone. Probably so we could not track her."

"She knows."

"And she listens."

Milena gasped.

"Milena. Do not make this harder than it is. Come home. We will discuss this. It is not what it seems. Bring your friend. The bodyguard. Yes, I remember him. And don't think about bothering the policewoman. This is family business. Yes?"

And her mother added, "Mila. If you are listening, please. Your father's life depends on it."

The line went dead on her mother's side, but from the breathing on the phone, she knew Ivan had kept the line open. Waiting. Seconds ticked by, along with her pulse.

Her gaze, which had been glued to the phone, lifted to meet Sean's, briefly. His wide eyes were more curious than shocked. She peered over at Nash. His fist was around the phone.

"Careful." She laid her hand around his. "If you break it, I can't replace it."

The only prototype of the Telek and it laid in his hand.

"He's not hanging up," Nash muttered.

Then a zap of panic hit her in the chest. "Hang up."

She hit the end button and tried to breathe.

"What?" Sean asked.

How could she have been so stupid!

"He knows where we are." She moved to grab her things. "We have to leave. Now."

Heart wrenching, another person pulled into her web of trouble. She blinked back the tears of fear and frustration.

"He can trace us through that?"

Smart guy. Stupid girl.

She swallowed back the injustice of it all.

"If he knew we were listening, I wouldn't put it past him."

"How?" Nash asked.

"You wish for me to explain technical stuff right now? We need to leave before Anton, or the other guy, shows up again." She glanced at Sean. "And it would be best for you to not be here either. I'm sorry."

She winced. The words physically hurt her to admit.

"Wow." Sean pressed the heels of his hands to his eyes. "Seriously? You can trace someone through a tapped call?"

"Yes. Now let's go!" Milena needed to get out of there. Fast. Her skin had gotten too tight for her body. Her palms became sweaty. She had her bag and was heading for the door as the two men finished processing. She was taking off without them.

Ivan's words flared up in her mind. Don't go to the police. A family thing.

Would he still be looking at the airport?

She reached for the doorknob. Her legs went weak. Her mother's voice on the phone made her suddenly dizzy. Plus the fact she hadn't slept a wink.

As she fell, two muscular arms enclosed around her. "Whoa there, Mila. I've got you."

She clung to him. To those arms that had always been there to hold her and support her. Her legs gave way, and her vision blurred. He held her up. "Take a deep breath. I'm here."

She breathed him in deep. Masculinity. Momma Shirley's red sauce. Spices. All Nash. She closed her eyes to ward off the spinning.

"You sure she doesn't need caffeine?" Sean asked.

"It'll only make it worse."

She fell apart, tears dampening her lashes as she tried to hold it together. Too much.

Not her mother, too.

"My father is in danger, isn't he? It's my fault."

Nash pulled her tighter in his arms. "You don't know that. Besides, we'll figure this out. I told you. We're in this together." His broad chest against her back. She leaned her head back against his shoulder. He pressed his cheek against hers, and she couldn't seem to hold it together any longer.

10

Sean agreed to return Big Ollie's car. The entire situation had gone from a sickening feeling in the pit of her stomach to heartburn. Nash borrowed Sean's Jeep and promised her a hot cup of tea when this was over. She would have had breakfast but, pressing her hand to her queasy stomach, had politely declined.

All Milena wanted to do was get this done and have it be over.

Easier said than done, she sighed. Nash held her hand. He kept a hold of it during the drive. When they arrived, he came around and opened the door for her. His hand slid back in place with hers as if they were always meant to be joined that way. She glanced around the parking lot. They'd driven around the police station, parked at a nearby business, and walked the rest of the way. What if Ivan had someone watching the station?

She let her hair down. Humidity would soon turn it to a curling frizzy mass by noon. *Welcome to the wild spring weather of Baltimore.* She tried to put on a smile. A fake one to mask the growing anxiety building inside her. *You're too headstrong to be afraid.* Nash leaned his shoulder into hers. She caught a whiff of his bacon sandwich and that Old Spice he wore. It should have relaxed her, but the calm was a long time in coming.

"Are you sure this is a good idea?" Since when had she gone from running to him, from him, then trusting him?

Twenty-four hours and almost getting killed had a way of twisting things around.

"He won't think you're ballsy enough to do it," Nash said.

"My father? What if—?" She couldn't finish the sentence. It choked her up inside and scratched at the rawness already there. Just when she thought she'd emptied the waterworks on Nash back in the apartment, she found she had a little more in reserve. Typical female, she could hear her father scolding her. There was no place for tears in a situation such as this. Ballsy. That was Nash's word. That's what she needed to be, and she could.

She was Milo Borghese's daughter.

Inside the precinct, powerful waves of coffee scents and something foul made her nose twitch. Caffeine, even with the repercussions of a migraine later, seemed a better option than what she was about to go through.

"I hope you"re right," she murmured.

"Me, too," Nash said.

At the counter, a police officer glanced over at them. "Can I help you?"

"We're looking for Detective Thompson."

"One second." The officer moved away.

Milena shivered. She should have put on a light cardigan or a jacket. Nash must have felt her reaction. He let go of her hand and slid his arm around her waist, pulled her against him.

"Maybe she's not here. We could speak to someone else," she said, but then the woman in question strolled out around a desk in the back and walked toward them.

"Miss Borghese. You finally decided to come in and make your statement?"

Gina put her hands on her hips, in full uniform with her baton resting against her thigh. "Did you find the body? Or does this have to do with your condo break-in?"

"It has to do with two men trying to kill me in a parking garage and the man behind it."

Gina glanced at Nash. Her brow hiked into her forehead.

Milena licked her upper lip and tried to look past the woman's connection with Nash. He said they were friends. Milena had no right to feel possessive of him. They hadn't seen each other in months. Either way, it shouldn't bother her as much as it did.

Gina didn't like her.

Milena couldn't blame her. The feeling was mutual.

Putting feelings aside, Milena focused on the reason they'd come here. The sooner this was over, the sooner they could move on to other things, like finding out if Ivan had kidnapped her father and what exactly that conversation with her mother had been about.

Her chest caved in a little. Her mother mingled in social circles of lunch dates and spa outings with some of the most influential women in Baltimore. She traveled. Often. Homesick for Russia and family that Milena's father couldn't ever return to see. What if someone had put her mother up to this and Ivan was helping, and she'd misunderstood?

No. And nor would she mention this to the woman in uniform standing in front of her. Things had gotten too personal, too fast. Complicated, and Milena had allowed it to happen. Just as she'd almost allowed Nash to kiss her last night, or had it been her imagination, and she'd just wanted him to kiss her? One thing she wasn't about to share with anyone, especially Nash's friend.

Just one more secret.

One more lie, but not.

"You have a personal issue with me. I understand this. If you can find someone else who would listen and help with my situation, I'd appreciate it," Milena said.

She would have suggested Officer Brumel.

Gina narrowed her eyes. She wore her mascara thick and her suspicion even thicker.

"Who says I won't help you?"

Detective Thompson oozed of incredulity. Could she see right through Milena and read her mind? No woman liked to have another woman step in when it came to getting in the middle of a close friendship. If that was indeed what it was between Gina and Nash.

Milena wouldn't be that woman. She needed Nash. She got him stuck in this because of her, and when this was over, Milena would be the one to walk away this time.

"I believe it is written all over your face," Milena said.

"She has a point, Gina. You don"t look thrilled to see us," Nash said.

Gina tilted her hip, leaning toward her baton. "I don"t know what you"re talking about. I believe you said something about men and shooting. When did this take place?"

"Late yesterday afternoon, close to evening," Nash said, unaffected by her sharp tone.

"Why didn't you call the police then?" Gina asked.

"We were trying to stay alive," Nash said.

Gina tilted her chin. "I see you had no problem finding her."

Those lashes might have been smothered with liquid eyeliner, but they couldn't keep Milena from noticing the hurt in Gina's eyes. One more thing to twist her stomach and make her out as the terrible person in all this. The poor woman had deeper feelings for Nash than he acknowledged.

She had bigger problems. Ivan. Her mother. Her father.

Milena pinched her nose. It helped to keep her in focus. "I hid in his truck."

"Runaway bride?" Gina shook her head. "You know, if you don't want to marry the guy, you should say so. Unless you have some actual evidence."

Nash cleared his throat. "Two men shot at us. I disarmed one, and I left the other in the garage after I blocked the door of the stairwell to keep him from coming after us. My truck is parked over in the Harbor Parking Garage. I think you'll find it's got a bullet in the side fender."

Gina's eyes, a shade of dark green, widened slightly. "Follow me."

Nash placed his hand against the middle of Milena's back and pressed her forward. Warmth radiated in that spot, heating emotions she tried to leave tucked away.

She couldn't think of one man while promised to another even if that man had sent men to kill her. And Nash had some strings still attached she didn't want to get further entangled in.

Milena kept her chin tilted up, following Gina, and grateful for Nash at her side.

Gina took her into a room with a table and two chairs.

"Have a seat, won't you?" Gina indicated a nearby chair.

Milena leaned closer to Nash. "Why do I feel like I'm being held for doing something I didn't do?"

Was she the victim or the perpetrator? In Gina's eyes, she was, no doubt, the latter. Milena took a deep breath, silently praying for God to help Gina see the truth in their situation and to blind Ivan's watchmen to keep him from finding out she'd come here. If anything happened to her father—Milena tried to push it all down so it wouldn't over-come her.

"It'll be okay," Nash tried to reassure her.

Gina gave him a long look. "I'll get Officer Lee. He'll record your statement, and we'll do what we can from there. Did you know the men who were shooting at you?"

"I recognized one of them."

Gina nodded. "Do you know why they were trying to harm you?"

"They want something they think I have."

"Which would be?" Gina asked.

"Should I have brought a lawyer?" Milena asked.

"I believe Gina needs to get Officer Lee," Nash said.

Gina scowled. "Yeah. Give me a minute."

Milena turned away, but in the glass against the wall, she could see the reflection of Gina tilting her head and motioning for Nash to follow her.

"I'll be right back. I just need to check something."

Milena glanced over her shoulder at him and decided to keep her opinion to herself. She pressed a hand to her heart to keep it from jumping out of her chest. What other choice did she have than to trust him? Where else did she have to go?

A moment later, Nash came back in.

"That was quick," she said.

"What's that supposed to mean?"

Milena walked up to him. Touched his cheek, tilted it from one side to the other. He had a night's scruff on his chin.

"What are you doing?" Nash asked.

Milena stepped away, too tempted to cup his firm jaw and pull those lips down to hers in a reunion of sorts. She shrugged and turned away. "Guess she doesn't wear lipstick."

She meant it to make him laugh, a snide remark to ease the tension of being trapped and waiting for them to come back so she could spill her guts. She pressed a hand over her lips. She might spill them anyway.

Nash spun her around, held her at arm's length. "I've already told you Gina is a friend. Why won't you believe me?"

"You did." Milena grinned. "But it's too fun to see you flustered."

Nash's eyes narrowed. "Fun? You think this is fun?"

"No," her voice trembled. "It's far from fun."

She should have gone straight to the airport and flown anywhere to get away from Ivan. Away from Nash. Then Nash would think her a coward, just as he did her father. He would have been right. She should have confronted him a long time ago instead of nursing her broken heart and allowing her father and Ivan to determine her future. At the time, she hadn't wanted to face another rejection. How could she have known he wouldn't have turned her away, or it had been Nash, not her father, who made him leave Borghese Technology and her all those months ago?

She should have had more trust in him, but right now, she couldn't afford to have him walk away from her again.

All her life, her parents had taught her to trust in someone she couldn't see. To have faith in God and accept His will in her life. She trusted her father, and he had chosen Ivan. She trusted her heart, and it had chosen Nash. Both choices had brought her pain.

No matter what, she'd do what she needed to do. She couldn't trust anyone.

Because sometimes you don't always get what you want. Her mother's words, not hers.

Nash's thumbs rubbed against her arms, sending spiraling zings of static electricity, which made the fine hairs on her arms rise. And if that weren't enough, those narrowed eyes, darkened, roping her in. She'd seen them look like that before, right before he kissed her.

"Am I interrupting?" Gina asked from the doorway.

Nash's jaw clenched, and he stepped back. "You can trust Gina."

If only she could believe him. As soon as this was all over, they could both go back to their lives. She'd managed to survive these past months without him. She could move on when this was over. Even if it meant giving in to Ivan to ensure her family wasn't harmed.

"Can we just get this over with?" Milena asked.

Gina swung out her arm, inviting Milena to walk ahead of her. The sooner she got the paperwork finished and this statement to Nash's girlfriend, the sooner she could get out of here.

"Ever find that dead body?" Gina asked.

"His name is—was Benson. He works for my father. He's a driver. And I know what I saw."

Milena wouldn't sit. Not for the life of her. She had too much pent-up energy pouring out as she relived the moment Benson had turned and demanded the files, the

Telek. She blinked away the desperate face in her mind of a company driver turned feral over a piece of digital technology. And on top of it all, Ivan had sent Anton after her. Would he have shot her?

"Two men tried to kill me yesterday in a parking garage."

"So you've already said." Gina sat on the corner of the table.

A man, shorter, dark cropped hair, and having spent too much time out in the sun walked in. "I'm ready to take your statement, Miss Borghese "

"Just start from the beginning." Nash's hand was on hers again. Anywhere else, without an audience, she would have leaned back further into his touch. She did a little. Maybe a part of her wanted to spite the other woman. Bitterness churned in her gut. Nash had walked away from her. She hadn't chased him. It wouldn't have seemed ladylike.

There was still a chance she might end up Mrs. Yaroslav depending on how it all went down in the next forty-eight hours.

"Tell us again about the dead man."

Milena huffed, rolled her eyes, and started from the beginning.

11

By the time the police finished questioning Milena, recorded her statement and had the papers ready for her to sign verifying what she had said was correct, the process ate up a few hours of their morning. Nash had grabbed a cup of coffee Gina offered him.

He stood back, waiting for her to finish with Officer Lee as Gina rolled back her shoulders and approached him. "It's almost lunch. If you want to stick around, we can head to Shirley's together."

"Not going to make it. I don't think Milena should be alone with Ivan sending his men out to search for her."

"Which is why the chief sent Officers Brumel and Lee to monitor her at her place while we investigate further. We can swing by and check on your truck in the parking garage and look for evidence there."

Milena hadn't told Gina about the phone call. As much as he wanted to tell her, it wasn't his place. Would he have done the same thing in her place?

"I can't. Tell the others I'll catch up next week. Ollie

will understand. Sean will return his car if he hasn't already, and once this over—" Gosh, he didn't know.

Gina shifted her weight and stayed her distance. "Nash, you should know we're only taking this more seriously because I trust you. But are you sure this isn't a spat between lovers? Or a power struggle in the family business? There is no body, and no proof. I'm worried about you. I've been praying for you since the day we met. I know you have a past with her, and it hurt you. I don't want to see you get hurt again. Please, don't get involved any deeper. I've seen cases like this. If it's what you say it is, this is more than a security issue or helping a friend. She's in danger."

Didn't he know that? Hadn't he always known that?

And he'd walked away.

Nash shook his head "Gina. I walked away once, and that was a mistake. I appreciate your prayers, and I hope you'll keep Mila in them, too. She didn't ask for this." Nor had she asked him to leave.

If anyone had been a coward, it had been him.

Milena walked out along with Officer Lee. "I think we are done here."

She wrung her hands together. Her purse hung between her hands. "Officer Lee has offered to take me home, and he and Officer Brumel will watch over the place, but I politely tried to explain to them it wasn't necessary. I have no intention of returning home today."

"You shouldn't leave town," Gina said.

Milena took her purse and slipped the strap over her shoulder and tucked her hair back out of the way. "I'm not."

"And just where do you think you are going?" Gina asked.

Milena had paled since they'd entered the police

station. He remembered she hadn't eaten at Sean's. Probably, she'd been too nervous. He knew her, just as he knew Gina would press and not let this go.

He spoke up for her, "I'm taking her to her mother."

Not a lie.

They both knew Milena's mother, Zoya, was involved. It might look like she was the one calling the shots, but they had yet to find out the truth.

And the truth will set you free.

One could hope.

For Milena's sake, he did. He *really* did.

Nash moved away from Gina and offered Milena his arm. "Ready? Your mother probably has lunch waiting."

For her, but for them, Nash would take her to a place and see the color returned to her cheeks. He'd make her blush if he had to. Her deathly white pallor disturbed him.

Milena took hold of him. "Thank you again. I appreciate you taking the time to look into this matter. As you are now aware, you can understand why I won't be going home at this time, and I assure you I will be safe in the shelter of my mother's home."

She'd put on that air of professionalism Nash had witnessed so many times seeing her working in the office and social events. He wanted the more casual, shield-free Milena back.

"Something else happens or comes up, I'll call you," Nash told Gina.

Her lips pressed, thinned, and then she said, "See that you do, but just to be safe, we'll still have guys driving around Miss Borghese's place and yours."

"Thank you," Milena said, tugging on Nash for them to go.

Outside on the street she sighed. He didn't need to ask what that was about.

"Where are we off to now?" she asked.

Nash grinned at her. "To one of your favorite places."

———————

Inside the Shake Shack. Nash sat a strawberry shake down in front of her, along with a double cheeseburger. During the time Nash worked for her father, this had been her guilty pleasure once a week.

She'd only ever shared it with Nash.

Those late nights after work, not wanting another salad, she indulged in a shake and a burger.

Nash sat across from her, leaned in on his elbows. "Eat up."

Going to the police station had drained her. Even with the emptiness leaving her hollow, she had to figure out her next steps. She sucked on her shake, savoring the straw-berry taste at the tip of her tongue.

"I think we should go to see your mother." All the sugar he sucked down in his salted caramel shake had gone to his head. First the police, then this?

"My mother is the last person I want to see right now."

"Exactly why you should pay her a visit."

"You have only met my mother a handful of times. She'll tie me up and cart me to Holy Trinity and marry me off to Ivan in the blink of an eye. You heard her on the phone."

"You didn't mention the call to the police."

"I didn't want them arresting my mother." She stuffed her face with a giant bite of burger to keep from saying more. Her mother would gasp at seeing her eat this way.

The scent of grease and fruity ice cream made her stomach growl. Famished, she ignored Nash and polished off her meal.

She could have used a second, and as if he could read her mind, he pushed his closer to her. "You don't fool me, Milena Borghese. I saw the act you put on with Gina and the others at the police station, and I've seen you handle others at work, but here it's just you and me."

"Almost like old times." She took a deep gulp of her shake. The sudden cold went straight to her head, and she winced. Brain freeze. Looking at his burger and at her fries, she slid him the fries. "Except back then, it was your job."

He picked one up and said, "Taking you home, coming here, I was off duty. It was never my job."

Off duty.

Off limits.

She sighed and bit into the burger. Around them, people stood in line for food, the kitchen called out orders, and a group of people sat behind them. They all looked like they were the type who needed to escape offices and cubicles for a while. She couldn't blame them. There were days she just needed to step away for enough minutes to take a breather before going back and getting through the day.

A man in a T-shirt caught her attention. He glanced up from a laptop—not that Shake Shack was the place to sit in the corner and work with all the noise, people, and food during an afternoon. His thick-rimmed glasses held a reflection in the corner.

Milena almost forgot to chew before she swallowed and started choking.

"You okay?" Nash would have lifted both her arms and patted her on the back. How embarrassing!

"I'm fine. You were saying?"

She tried not to glance at the guy again.

Nash glanced around too, his gaze coming back in her direction. "Your mother. I think we should go there."

"I think we should go back to the office. My father might have left a clue. Or perhaps go back to the Oyster House here in town. Benson's body couldn't have disappeared."

"Or he might still be alive," Nash pointed out with a fry, his gaze wandering around again as a new trio of customers came through the door.

"I know what I saw."

"Sometimes, things aren't always the way they appear."

"He couldn't have survived." She trembled again, seeing his face, the way his eyes widened and the pupils took over, sending the man into eternal darkness.

"And your mother couldn't be involved with the wrong people?"

Not the Zoya Borghese she knew. Not the mother who led the PTO at her school and had dresses designed for her prom. Even at this moment, her mother probably had a book of dresses and formal wear, along with a seating arrangement made up for Milena's big day. A day that, once Milena had decided to move on and accept her fate, wouldn't be so bad. From the day Ivan came into her life, he felt off to her. Not because of Nash, or so she first thought. It wouldn't have worked out between them.

The guy with the glasses seemed to move his mouth, and Milena noticed no one around him. She couldn't see his screen. She narrowed her gaze, caught the reflection in his glasses again.

How could she have missed it the first time?

"Those aren't ordinary glasses."

"What?" Nash said as if she'd spoken a foreign language.

"Don't look, but the man near the trash receptacles had thick-rimmed glasses. He's videoing us. Someone is watching us."

Nash lifted the last of his fries, three at a time, and ripped off a big bite. He chewed, keeping his eyes on her. "And you know this because?"

She gave him the most flirtatious smile she could conjure. "They're Borghese. I helped in the design."

"You stay here. I'll have a chat with our friend." Nash rose.

Milena reached across, put her hand on his. She tilted her head and fluttered her lashes. "And risk making a scene?"

"We need to know who is watching us." Nash leaned in, popped the last of his fries in his mouth. The man had the most sensual chew style she'd ever seen.

"Whoever is watching us, they'll know where we are, and Yaroslav will have men on the way."

Milena peered over at the man. He turned his head, but she'd caught him looking first. Tempted to go over to him and find out where he'd gotten those glasses, she said, "He doesn't seem familiar, but that's not to say he couldn't be testing the glasses. We haven't put them on the market yet."

"Are you finished?" Nash asked.

"Almost." She finished her shake. Who knew when she'd get another one? While patting her lips, a sharp pain hit the center of her forehead. She'd drunk that too fast. Ignoring the tingle of brain freeze, everything in her screamed for her to jump up and run. She forced her movements into slow motion. "I'll be right back."

Nash frowned. "I am coming with you."

"There are some places a girl must go alone," she said, sliding out of her seat with a wink. "I won't be long."

He grabbed her arm, put her nose to nose with him. "What are you doing?"

She licked her lips. Her gaze dropped to his mouth. "I have no idea."

Whatever she'd been thinking seconds before vacated her mind. Time. Oh yes. She meant to buy them some time.

"We should walk out of here together."

"I need to use the restroom." That part of her body signaling her brain, she needed to go.

Go now.

It took only a gentle tug, his lips fusing to hers in a simple mind-blowing kiss. He could have made it more, and as she opened to invite him to do just that, he nibbled at the corner of her lip and pulled away.

"One minute. Make it fast. I'll be at the door waiting," he whispered in her ear. To anyone looking, it would appear innocent and sweet, rather than a plot of escape.

She straightened, pulled her wobbly legs back underneath her. "I won't—I won't be long."

The guy with glasses had shut down his laptop. He reached for a drink, and his face turned away from her.

She headed for the ladies' room. Thankful there wasn't a line, she did what she needed to do and stepped back out in record time. The guy with the glasses stood waiting for her. His long sleeve shirt unbuttoned revealed a solid white T-shirt.

He pushed up his spectacles and grinned. "I have a message for you."

"Do you know who I am?"

His grin broadened. "I know who you are, Milena Borghese."

She peered around him. Where was Nash?

"Your friend will be here, momentarily. I believe he has gotten distracted. However, I must say you are more lovely in person than on camera."

"Your message?"

"Did you enjoy your shake?"

She put her hand over her stomach. "Who are you? What do you want?"

"Patience, if one holds enough, eventually pays off." His hand snaked out and took hold of her arm. "We don't have much time."

"What makes you think I'm going anywhere with a stranger?"

He tilted down his glasses. "You're a little too old for the whole stranger warning."

"And you're too old to be a smarty-pants."

He laughed. "I'm smart enough to have people in the right places. I also know how much you love strawberries and shakes. How's that head feeling?"

"My head?" She reached up and touched her head. "What? There was something in my shake?"

"Your boyfriend won't have as big of a headache as you will, but if you come with me now, I promise to make it better before you suffer."

"How dumb do you think I am?"

A sharp pain trickling down the center of her forehead said differently. "It was the strawberry shake."

"Caffeine powder. Shall we?"

She glanced over her shoulder. Where was Nash when she needed him most?

12

Nash woke up in the back of an ambulance.

Groggy, he rubbed his jaw. It throbbed like someone had given him a good uppercut. He couldn't remember getting in a fight. He remembered sitting at the Shake Shack. Milena. Milena! He sat straight up. A woman pressed her hand to his chest. "Easy there, buddy," she said.

Another guy turned, dressed in an EMT uniform. "Hey, he's awake."

"What happened?" He blinked. His head hurt. He pinched his nose and waited for the stars swimming in front of his eyes to disappear.

"You pass out often?" The woman took his wrist, checked his pulse. Her grip tightened in anticipation of him pulling his arm away.

"No. Where is she?" Warning bells were going off in his head.

Milena tricked him again. He pressed the heel of his hand against one eye.

"Who?"

Nash turned his head, looked at the male EMT. "The woman I was with. Where is she?"

"You were alone at the table. You'd been there for a while. The owner got concerned and called us."

He'd gotten the food.

They'd talked about her mother.

The guy with the glasses. Those were Borghese design. He threw his legs off the gurney. "Whoa there, pal. Hang on. You've been out for a while."

"A while?" Nash tried to shake off the hands, holding him down. "How long?"

"We don't know. Take it easy."

Nash grabbed the guy by the shirtfront. "How. Long."

"A couple of hours, at least," the woman said. Her cornrows were tinged with gray. "We'll get a blood sample at the hospital and figure out what's going on."

"No need," Nash said. "I appreciate the concern, but I'll decline."

"One too many last night?"

Nash slid off the gurney. "What are you saying?"

"You have any medical conditions? Narcolepsy?" the woman asked.

"No. Can I go?" Nash asked.

"I can't hold you here. Normally, I'd advise a trip to the hospital. Next time, go home and sleep before you grab a bite to eat."

Nash exited the ambulance, which was parked on the street in front of the shake joint. Gina leaned against her car, arms crossed, and legs crossed at the ankles. "I knew you wouldn't let them take you to the hospital."

"How did you find me?"

"The call came in to us. I was the closest, so I came to check it out."

"What about lunch?" He cupped the back of his head, trying to make sense of the time he lost. Where was Milena?

She wouldn't have skipped out on him again.

Would she?

"Lunch was over an hour ago, Nash." She pushed away from the police SUV. "Question is, what happened here?"

"We had lunch."

"Some lunch." She rested her hand on her belt.

Nash shook his head, hoping to rattle pieces together. "Have you seen her? She went to the restroom."

"I bet she did," Gina said.

"She's not here?"

"Haven't seen her."

Nash ground his teeth together.

He'd ordered the food. Gave her his burger. The guy wearing glasses.

She'd gone with him. Willingly?

"We have to find her."

He had watched her go to the restroom. Stood when his head got heavy, and his eyes burned with a need to close them for a minute. He put his head down.

The man with the glasses. Milena.

She wouldn't have—

Hands on her hips, Gina gave him a sympathetic look. "Face it, Nash. She's not here. You've been played. If not for the bullet hole in the side of your truck, I'd say she'd done a superb job. She could have hired the two men to chase you in the parking garage."

"You're loving this, aren't you?" Nash asked.

"I'm not trying to rub it in." Gina reached for his hand. "Have you forgotten what she cost you?"

"I don't need you to keep reminding me. It wasn't Milena's fault I lost my job. That's between her father and me."

"So, you forgive her? Even if she just drugged you and ran off again?"

Gina was one to talk about forgiveness. She hadn't spoken to her sister in years, but forgiveness wasn't always about going right back where you were when someone hurt you.

He could see by the deep concern on her face she cared. Like all his friends, none of them wanted anyone to get hurt.

He squeezed her hand, reassuring. "It's me she should forgive, and I don't think she drugged me. I know she didn't."

Nash took a few steps away from the curb while the ambulance driver shut the doors and prepared to drive away.

"Then what happened?"

"He has her." Nash balled his hand into a fist.

"Are you sure?" Gina reached for the walkie clipped to her chest.

"Has to be him."

"Yaroslav."

"Who else?" Nash went to take a step and wobbled. "I need to find her. He wants—"

Gina caught him by the arm. "Whoa there, big guy. We need to get whatever that is out of your system first. We have guys patrolling around her house and looking into the situation. Her story is paper-thin without a car or a body, but I checked out your truck. There's a bullet hole in the side door."

He gritted his teeth to keep from saying, "I told you so."

Bryon and Jaylene came walking toward him.

"I called your brother," Gina said.

———

She got in the car, a black Mercedes. As Milena slid in, the electric locks clicked into place. He sat beside her. She tried to think if she should know him. It hurt to think. She pressed a few fingers to her temple. "You promised me a cure if I came with you."

She took quick breaths, in through the nose, out through the mouth. "How do you know so much about me?"

"One thing at a time." He snapped his fingers. "Benson, Miss Borghese's drink."

"Benson?" A slow cold droplet of realization trickled down her spine. She squinted against the onset of a headache. So far, the sharp pain from before had let up. Maybe it wouldn't be so bad. But if he had put a shot of caffeine in her drink, he could have set her up to be out for days. Soon even the light would hurt, and she refused to close her eyes and be at the mercy of this stranger.

A hand reached back with a water bottle. Black skin. She followed the arm to verify seeing his face. Benson. Alive.

"How?" she murmured. "I saw you die."

"And he would have if not for the bullet-proof vest under his suit."

"There was blood." It gave her nightmares.

"A scratch," Benson said.

"I have to give it to your betrothed. He is a determined man. I can see why your mother chose him."

Everything halted in her head. Reaching for the drink, in slow motion, she watched the stranger put his hand in his pocket, pulling out a plastic pill case. He flipped it open and offered her the two little round white pills inside.

At least she'd been right about Ivan.

But her mother?

She'd have to wait and find out once they got to their destination.

It hurt to think. *Please don't let this turn into a full-blown headache.*

She could barely wrap her brain around all this now.

"Where next, Mr. Callahan?" Benson asked.

Milena sank back in the seat. Callahan. She'd heard that name. Hadn't she? A conversation. Her head filled with a quiet ache from the base of her neck.

"Locust Point. You know the house."

He extended his hand with the pills toward her. "I'd take these before it gets any worse."

She worried about Nash. Had they done the same thing to him? Of course not, the man could chug caffeine like there was no tomorrow and still sleep at night. Would he try to find her this time?

She doubted it, even if her heart wanted to think he would.

Taking the pills, she swallowed and took a swig of water before she couldn't think at all. Callahan knew too much about her.

And Benson.

Alive.

She needed to find a way to inform the police.

Would they believe her? Gina would use this against her.

She'd seen him die. The man had shot him. Not Calla-han. Not Anton. She closed her eyes, pressed her fingers to her eyes. Think, Milena. Think. Who was the other man working with Anton?

Not as important as the man beside her.

Callahan. She'd heard that name. Where?

Then her eyes snapped open, and she almost dropped the water bottle on the leather seat.

"You're Roland Callahan."

"Very perceptive." He grinned. "At last, a face to put with the name, am I right?"

"You're not at all who I pictured."

He laughed. "Let me guess. You expected me to be as old as your father?"

"At least late thirties, if not early forties," she admitted.

"Ah, but we are close in age, you and I." He snapped the pillbox shut and slid it in his pocket again. "I believe our birthdays are even in the same month."

Milena chewed on her lip. Roland Callahan ran Boyko Technology. It had impressed her father how someone Callahan's age could rise in the industry so fast. A man in his late twenties should still be tinkering in his garage or working in technology labs alongside her.

The guy was full of crap. She could see it in his eyes glistening behind the thick lenses of his glasses. His hair swept over, except for the cowlick, which made the middle stand up. His straight nose had never been broken, and Milena doubted the man had ever burnt the tip of his fingers or calloused them in perfecting any of his inventions.

Roland Callahan created nothing. He just stole from others.

"This is all just a setup."

Callahan grinned. "Your father always said you were smart. Not very, or you wouldn't have pulled the security guard into this. Although knowing your history with the man, I can't say I'd blame you for trying to rekindle lost love."

"Leave Nash out of this."

"Nash Dunford. Former chief of security for your father's company. Put his nose in where it didn't belong. Made assumptions. Wrong ones. And if that wasn't bad enough, he overstepped the bounds and got a little too personal with the boss's daughter."

He paused, glanced out the window, then looked back at her. "Shall I go on? Would you like to know where he grew up? That he failed European history in ninth grade? He went into the reserves, never fully committed to the Navy. A guy who can't commit isn't much of a prospect, don't you agree?"

Milena capped the water, set it between them. She would have rather thrown it in his face. Then it occurred to her. He had no gun. She'd gone with him, and his trick had worked. How long had he been spying on her?

"So you paid someone to look into backgrounds. Am I to be impressed?"

"You disappoint me. After the incident yesterday, where Benson failed to obtain his objective, I expected more of a fight from you. Do you often flee when things get tough?"

"I do when someone is trying to kill me." She clasped her hands together. She refused to curl up, close her eyes, or even touch the spot of her neck that blossomed into a full foundation for the ache brewing in her head.

"You were fortunate Benson was there to serve as a distraction. I believe the intent was to scare you enough to get information."

Benson looked at her through the rearview mirror.

She bit her lip to keep from gasping. His face had black bruises and a cut under his eye.

"I saw him get shot."

"Stunned him, you mean."

She'd seen blood hasn't she?

His face screwed up tight in shock and pain. His eyes dulled. Her mind pounded as she tried to recall yesterday morning. She ran. It all seemed like a blur.

"All that matters is I get what was promised to me."

It clicked into place as she glanced out the tinted windows. "You're the one buying our trade secrets from Ivan, aren't you?"

"Is your head feeling better?" he asked, avoiding her question. No matter, she knew the answer. Should have figured this a long time ago.

"What do you care?" she muttered.

"I care a great deal." Callahan reached over and took her hand. Cool over the top of her damp palm, he squeezed. "We're here."

13

Locust Point.

A house with tall white columns and brick exterior came into view. Milena watched as Benson pulled them up in front of the grand house. "Why are we here?"

"Your father is expecting you."

"I think you have the wrong house." Her parents lived in a gated community, much like this one, but among the middle class. It had been the house she grew up in, and to her mother's dismay, her father had refused to move even though they could have afforded a grand mansion to live in.

Benson came around, opened the car door for her, and she hesitated. "Go on. I'm right behind you."

Callahan slid across the back seat and got out behind her. He fixed his glasses and took her by the arm.

Neither man appeared armed. She could run. Where?

Callahan leaned in and whispered, "The pain reliever was just a suppressant until I could get you here for the full cure."

Her temples sent out pulsing beacons of impending headache symptoms.

Milena sighed.

She walked up the stone stairs to the home's entrance. Inside the foyer, Callahan said, "Welcome to my home. Benson shall get you a drink. Your father awaits in my study."

"If you've hurt him——"

Callahan slid his hand over her back and pressed her forward. "Don't make idle threats. They're very unbecoming for a lady."

Her flats clicked across the marble, and she caught glimpses of modern art on the walls. Industrial-type furniture told her the man had excellent taste.

His house decor style and the manner in which he spoke didn't match. What kind of trap had she fallen into?

Two pocket doors slid open for her to enter the den. On the far wall two enormous windows opened out over a manicured lawn. On either side of the windows, bookshelves took up the entire length of the walls. A couch, a desk, and a set of chairs sat around a geometric rug.

She took a step down into the room. "I thought you said my father was here."

The desk chair turned, and in it, Milo Borghese sat. "You found her."

"She was with the security guard."

Benson walked in and held out a drink to her.

"I'd drink that before your head feels any more wicked than it already does," Callahan said.

"You've been here all this time?" She stared at her father.

"Drink your drink, Mila. I know you have questions."

She took the drink, sipped it, then Callahan reached over and tipped it to make her gulp.

"It's better to drink it straight down."

A mixture of tomato juice and something bitter hit her tongue.

Her father watched. His expression filled with concern. But he sat there. Just sat there.

Milena shoved Callahan's hand away. She finished the drink and pushed the empty glass toward him. She moved closer to her father.

His skin turned the pallor of the white pillars outside.

"Did he kidnap you, too?" she whispered.

A faint smile etched on her father's face. His long, wrinkled face filled with more creases. "No. Roland has only been doing what I asked him."

"His company is putting our company out of business. He's stealing our creations."

Callahan's eyes twinkled as he stood back and took a seat in one of the empty chairs. Her father pointed to the other. "Take a seat."

"Are you ill?" She sat on the corner of her seat.

"In a manner of speaking," her father said, glancing at Callahan. "A moment alone with my daughter?"

Callahan rose. "I have a few other things to attend to."

Milena watched Callahan leave before turning to her father. He put his elbows on the desk, glass and metal and too modern for her father's taste. She could see right through it, but not him.

"Ivan is after the Telek. He's selling our secrets to Boyko. They tried to kill me!" Her voice rose, and trembled. She gripped the seat to keep her from jumping to her feet. Her nails cut into the vinyl.

"He's only doing what your mother has asked him to do."

"How is Mother involved in this?"

He put his hands together on the desk. "To fulfill the deal she made with Ruslan Yaroslav. A deal I didn't know about until last year when Yaroslav contacted me to pay the debt I owed him."

"For me to marry his son."

Her father nodded. His clothes were rumpled, which came as no surprise. He often went for days in his workshop in the same outfit. It upset her mother. Her father wore suit coats seldom. If he had one, he wasn't wearing it now. His tie hung loosely around his neck.

"That was part of it. To ensure I would follow on the other part of having Yaroslav gain from our silent partnership through your marriage, he used a past grievance of your mother's to ensure control."

"Did you know what Ivan was doing?"

"He was snooping. '

"Mother?" It tightened her gut and made it twist. Either way, her head still pounded.

"No." He leaned back and sighed. "Ivan is ambitious. He focuses on one thing."

And it wasn't her. Relief came short lived.

"Like father, like son. I'm sorry, Milena. I never wanted you to get trapped in this."

"And what exactly have you got me trapped in?" She clung to the chair, her head pounding harder, not easing as Callahan promised.

"Yaroslav can have Borghese. What I leave of it. Ivan can explain how he sold out the company. Your mother will find her extravagant lifestyle shall not last, but I need two things, Mila. Please."

She closed her eyes, pressed her hand against her head. Her sinuses blocked and she moaned. "You're leaving Mother."

"I've already left her."

She chewed on her lip for a moment, waiting for the wave of nausea to pass. "I went to the police."

"Good," her father said.

She heard him get up out of the chair. "Your head is hurting."

"Your friend's tactic didn't work." She took a deep breath in through her nose and blew it out her mouth. "You want the Telek."

"I can't let your mother have this one. I have been able to duplicate and make better designs from Borghese to Boyko. Roland has been good with that, but your mother sends the design beyond Yaroslav for the highest bid. I can't allow it."

Oh, the pain settled in. Callahan had been working with her father all this time. "You're working with Callahan."

It grated her heart.

"He worked as my intern and then my assistant."

"And working with me?" She sucked in a breath, still not able to open her eyes and look at him.

"You are my daughter, which is why I trust you to do the right thing. You will marry Ivan, and you will give me the Telek."

"I can't do that."

He took her by the hands. "Did you not hear what I said, girl?"

"Ivan sent Anton after me. He sent a man to try to kill me!" She winced. Raising her voice made her head pound harder.

Her father made a noise in this throat. "Foolishness. He would not do that."

"He did. Another reason I will not marry him."

"You will marry him. You will fulfill the marriage contract with Yaroslav. After a year, you leave him."

Milena felt sick. "No."

"She has a point. It's a messy pile of paperwork. I say forget the wedding, take the money and go on a cruise. All we need is the Telek, and we're in business."

She hadn't heard Callahan return.

"Mila," her father's voice pleaded.

"No. When I marry, it will be for life." She tried to look at him through squinted eyes.

"At least give us the Telek," Callahan said.

"I can't."

"Your headache isn't getting better?" her father asked. What little she could see through slit eyes, blurred. "Why isn't her headache getting better?"

"Where's the Telek?" Callahan said, closer. His voice drifted down from above her back.

"Find it yourself." She leaned back, the movement making her world wobble.

"It's with the boyfriend," Callahan said and laughed.

"Who?" Her father rose; he stepped away from her. "What man is this you speak of?"

"Her personal security guard."

"Is this true?" Milo Borghese asked her. "Did you go to that man after I let him go?"

She couldn't answer him. She covered her hands in her face and cried. The pressure and the pain, too much.

"This was not supposed to happen," her father hissed.

"Then you take care of her, and I'll take care of concluding our business deal and getting the Telek."

14

Nash had no choice but to go home and get his bearings. Whatever drug had been put in his shake, it messed with his head and dragged him down into la-la land. A few hours' nap turned into almost a day, and when he woke, he feared he'd failed Milena again.

But Yaroslav needed her. He needed to marry her if he wanted any future control over the company. But how badly did he need the Telek?

And would she cave and give it to him?

He rubbed his eyes at hearing his cell phone ring. He didn't remember laying it down by the bed or even plugging it in.

"Hello?"

The voices sounded familiar. Two of them started a conversation as if he didn't just answer one of them. Or both of them. As if they hadn't heard him. Then Yaroslav's voice came across the line, and Nash sat up, wide awake.

"You're late. I said I wanted it by Friday."

Nash didn't recognize this voice. It wasn't Milena's mother.

"There's been a complication. I assure you you will get the files and the prototype to complete our deal," said Yaroslav in his rough accent.

"Oh, I know I will," the other man laughed. "I've recently gained some added insurance."

Nash's heart about leaped out of his chest. Milena. This was the guy who'd taken Milena.

His fingers curled around his phone. His knuckles turned white.

"What's that supposed to mean?" Yaroslav asked.

Yeah, what's that supposed to mean?

He couldn't keep his emotions from tearing at his gut.

"I have something of yours. Have no worries, she is safe, and I'll return her to you when we make the trade."

"What of the money? That was the deal," Yaroslav said.

Nash wanted to reach through the phone and cuff the man. Bad.

"It should satisfy you enough to get your woman back. Unless she is no longer important to you?"

There was a silence, a strain that reached down into Nash and twisted at him. Painfully. The more it stretched; the more Nash had to regulate his breathing to keep his cool.

"She is important to me. You will put her on the line so I can hear from her she is there, and she is well," Yaroslav said.

Nash's heart skipped a beat. Had there been a way to trace the call? How had Milena done it? He pulled the phone away from his ear. Put it on speaker and fiddled with the screen. His breath caught in his lungs.

"I'm afraid she can't come to the phone, but I have a photo for you. It shall suffice." And the phone dinged. The guy on the line must have sent a text to Yaroslav, but it didn't come through to Nash's phone. He grimaced. How could he see where she was?

"You drugged her?" Yaroslav's voice hardened.

"No. But I have to say a girl who can't stand the slightest bit of caffeine is a con on the list of marriageable qualities."

Yaroslav growled. It brought Nash back to taking a deep breath. The guy had feelings for her. Nash still didn't like him. "Where is she?"

He hissed at the phone. A blue screen and a circling icon spun as it searched and tried connecting as he tapped on the app he hadn't noticed before on his phone.

"She's sleeping. Cuddled up in my bed. She should be right as rain for our dinner date. You will join us, won't you?"

"Of course," Yaroslav said. "Tell me the place."

Nash heard a soft knock on his door, it creaked open, and he held up his hand for whoever came in to remain silent.

"Thames Street Oyster House. Bring the Telek. I'll bring your date. Seven o'clock."

The line went dead. The circle continued to spin.

"Come on. Come on," Nash muttered. He shook his phone.

"Tell me where she is."

Then he tossed the phone, laid his head in his hands, and shook away the rest of the haze from his drug-induced sleep.

"Maybe Gina should have let them take you to the hospital. You're getting violent there, bro."

Nash glanced up at Bryon. "And they could have killed her."

His younger brother crossed his arms and frowned. "Seems like they tried to kill you. I know this is your thing, but maybe you should let it go. Let Gina and the police handle it. You're not a security guard anymore, and you're not a cop."

Nash eased off the bed. "I'm the only one who can help her. I'm not about to let her father or anyone else run me off this time."

"Glutton for punishment much?" Bryon asked.

"If Jaylene were in trouble, you'd do whatever you could no matter what to keep her safe, wouldn't you?"

Bryon nodded. "It's like that, is it?"

"Yeah. It's like that," Nash said, finally admitting without saying it aloud that he still was in love with Milena Borghese.

Bryon walked over, picked up Nash's phone, and touched the screen before Nash could stop him. He turned the phone around for Nash to see. "You always were bad with tech stuff. Can't figure how you ever got the job in the first place working for a tech company. It looks like both calls came from opposite sides of town. I say we split up and check them out." Bryon tossed the phone at Nash, and he caught it.

"Handy app you got there. I take it that one isn't available in the app store?"

"No, and you're not getting involved with this," Nash decided a cold shower and fresh clothes would help him get his brain cleared to go after these guys. He knew Yaroslav, but not the other one.

"I am if I say I am." Bryon widened his stance. His arms crossed, he lowered his head and stared at Nash.

They'd done that when they were kids, preparing for the tackle, but Nash could hear time ticking away in his head and an urgency to get a move on pressing him to go forward.

"You can't leave Jaylene."

"She's at work. She'll be fine," Bryon said.

Nash rubbed his face one more time. "Fine, but you don't go inside without me. I think I should pay a visit to Milena's mother. Maybe I can get some information that will help."

"And what about the other place where the call came from?"

Bryon could tell all that from looking at the app for a few seconds? Geez, Nash had to up his game in technology if he were to get Milena back safely.

And he prayed she was safe. Because if she wasn't, he didn't know what he'd do then. The guilt of not protecting her better felt like a hot rod burning at his side.

"Maybe I should drive by it, case it out after—"

"No." Nash held up his hand. "I know where to find Yaroslav."

"You're not going to show up at the meeting place?"

When Nash didn't answer, Bryon said, "You are."

"You don't have to help."

"You're right, but you've always been there for me, and I'm here for you. Someone's got to pull you out of trouble."

15

Nothing seemed out of the ordinary as Nash pulled up in front of the Borghese residence. They lived in one of the nicer neighborhoods on the West Side, a brick two-story with a well-maintained lawn.

He checked his watch, hoping to catch Milena's mother at home. He probably should have called first, but he couldn't risk losing the element of surprise. He prayed she hadn't gone out to brunch or lunch as most ladies did these days to escape the house. But something told him Milena's mother would have too many things on her mind to go out to lunch with friends.

He walked up to the door, glanced around, not surprised to find the camera in the corner of the door's frame, and his grin broadened. He put it on nice and wide when he rang the doorbell and stared up at the camera, so Zoya Borghese would let him in.

He could hear the footsteps. Heavy and in a hurry.

The next minute, the door wrenched open, and Nash blinked. Ivan Yaroslav stared coolly across at him.

"What are you doing here?"

Last time Nash had seen Ivan, the man wore a suit. Minus the jacket and the tie, and the twitch in his eye, Ivan held onto the door.

"I'd like to see Mrs. Borghese if she's here."

"Who is it?" a woman's voice shrilled from down the hall.

Ivan's muscles bunched in his arm under the sleeve of his shirt. "One minute."

He shut the door on Nash.

He whistled while he waited. His phone pinged, and he stepped out of direct view of the camera while he turned to check it. He couldn't read it. The text had come through the Telek, and the letters had changed to symbols, and the phone couldn't decode it. Had Ivan just texted someone? Or had someone texted Yaroslav?

Where was Bryon when he needed him?

The door flung open. Ivan took a deep breath, standing straighter, his eyes narrowed on Nash. "You can come in."

Nash bit back the retort at the tip of his tongue. He wanted to ask Yaroslav about his butler services, but that would have been a terrible idea. He couldn't afford to upset the man any more than he appeared. Not if he intended to find out anything here that could help lead him to Milena or finding out who the other guy Yaroslav was selling Borghese's trade secrets to.

He'd hand over this tech device in a minute if he thought it would get him to Milena faster. His heart had messed with his mind. Maybe Milena's father had been right all along when he told Nash he couldn't protect her because he cared about his client too much.

Yaroslav stepped back, and Nash entered the cool interior of the house. The entryway greeted him with smoky gray walls and a black framed mirror above a dark mahogany bureau.

"She waits in the living room."

Yaroslav walked in behind him. Having second thoughts of coming here alone, Nash entered the living room where an older version of Milena sat in a high-back chair and held a dainty cup of tea. Not at all the way he envisioned Milena in their future years. He tucked that away for now.

"I don't know you, but Ivan says you used to work for my husband." Her English was good, but the brogue of her voice slurred with her Slavonic heritage.

"Sit." She pointed to the chair across from him.

Nash waited until Yaroslav had taken a seat in the other high-back chair on the other side of Zoya.

"Standing doesn't intimidate me. Sit." She set her tea on the small table beside her. "Why are you here?"

Nash sat, just barely on the edge of the couch. "I was hoping you knew where Milena was."

Her dark hair was pulled back, twisted, and held by a gemstone comb. Her features were sharp, eccentric, where Milena's were softer. Zoya laid her hand on the arm of the chair, glanced over at Yaroslav. She spoke in Russian, her tone soft and calm.

Yaroslav responded in kind, and Zoya nodded.

"I do. Mr. Dunford, is it?"

A lot could be said in little time in a foreign language. He nodded.

"I have heard about you, both from my daughter and from her betrothed." Zoya waved a hand toward Yaroslav. "My husband fired you, did he not? And still, you do not stay away from my daughter. Why is that?"

"She asked me for help."

Yaroslav muttered something.

Zoya gave him a sharp look, then returned her gaze to Nash.

"She is much like her father. Flighty when stress hits the nerves. I assure you, she is fine. You may rest your conscience and go. Perhaps in a few weeks, she will invite you to the wedding."

He doubted that.

Yaroslav tapped his fingers on the side of his leg.

If this was the game they wanted to play, he'd play along. It was safer. He could see he wouldn't get any answers. He had to take the chance. For Milena.

"You've seen her? Talked to her?"

"Milena has gone to visit a friend. A weekend of pampering. This week has been—stressing," Yaroslav said. "As my future mother-in-law has said, the closer we get to the wedding, the more anxious my bride gets."

Anxious? You think?

Nash pulled back his shoulders. "And you'd know that because you saw her before she went to the friend's place? Or did she call you?"

Yaroslav held up his hand as Zoya's lips parted slightly.

"What is it you're looking to find out? The friend's name? The fact Milena lost her phone? I assure you she is fine. I would offer for you to call her, but it will take a few days for her new phone to arrive. Honestly, I don't believe it would be a good idea. I must ask you to stay away from my future wife."

Zoya's fingers gripped the chair for a second, enough for Nash to notice, then relaxed. "I appreciate your concern over my daughter, but now I must ask you to leave."

Nash didn't like the way Yaroslav got to his feet quickly. "I will give Milena your regards."

"Before or after you have one of your men kill her?"

Zoya gasped.

Yaroslav's jaw ticked.

Zoya reached over and laid her hand on Yaroslav's. "I can see how you are mistaken. Much has happened in the last couple of days."

Days, not hours, and more minutes slipped away, minutes that Milena remained in danger. It grated at him. Hard.

He opened his mouth to say they knew where Milena was, then clamped down to shut his mouth. They couldn't know he had the Telek. Not yet. Not when he had to get to Milena before they did.

"You sent men to kill her." He looked right at Yaroslav. "Ivan?"

Yaroslav shook his head. "You are mistaken. I would never hurt Milena. She is to be my wife."

"Tell it to the two guys who shot at us in a parking garage yesterday. Milena said the one guy was named Anton." He waited, watched for their reaction. Zoya paled.

"He would go to any lengths in *his* treachery." She pulled back her hand from Yaroslav. Curling it into a fist, she pounded it down on the arm of the chair.

"Who?"

Ivan scowled. He ranted to Zoya in Russian. She snapped back at him, and Nash rose, prepared to go. He wouldn't find anything out, and he needed to leave before the air got too thick for him to escape.

"Where are you going?" Zoya said, her English crisp.

"Listen. I get this is some messed-up family business you all got going, but Milena came to me, and as her friend, I intend to make sure she's safe. If she's with this friend, then have her call me. Until then, I'll go check with the police and see if they have any leads."

"Police?" Yaroslav said. "You called the police?"

"No, the restaurant did that when someone drugged me and Milena disappeared."

Zoya's eyes narrowed. "My husband sent you, didn't he? You're still in his employ?"

Before Nash could answer, the sound of his phone sending another text notification went off at the same time as Yaroslav's phone.

Yaroslav's eyes widened.

Nash sucked in a breath as Yaroslav reached around his back and pulled a gun. He leveled it at Nash. "He has the Telek."

"I don't know what you're talking about," Nash said.

"Maybe not, but you'll hand over your phone," Yaroslav said.

Zoya watched the men, patient. Her eyes gleamed a little too bright for Nash's comfort.

He decided it was better to try to distract them. He lifted his hands to signal surrender. "I work for Dunford Roofing. I haven't been on your husband's payroll for half a year. That's probably them checking in to see why I'm late getting back to the job."

Zoya reached over, took Yaroslav's phone. She tapped and read his message, then held out her hand for Nash's. "Then you won't mind if I read the message for you?"

His throat went dry. He'd let his foolish pride get between him and Milena for too long. If he handed over the phone, would they kill him?

A bead of sweat trickled down the back of his neck.

"Your phone, please?" Zoya persisted.

Reluctantly, Nash handed the woman his phone. He made sure to have the toggle at the top caught in his hand,

and the piece Milena had attached slipped into his palm. He kept his fist closed.

"He's lying," Yaroslav said. "Why else would he be hanging around Milena again?"

"She was afraid." And she had every right to be. "I would be too if my driver got killed in front of me, and the man she was to marry was selling out her family's company."

"You know nothing of which you speak," Zoya said, frowning at the phone. "What is your code?"

"May I?" It would give him a chance to move out of the range of Yaroslav's itchy trigger finger.

Yaroslav shrugged.

Nash took back the phone with his free hand. It vibrated in his hand. At the same time, Yaroslav gritted his teeth. Yaroslav reached in his pocket. "It's him."

"Answer it." Zoya leaned back, lifting a brow in Nash's direction. "The code. Enter it. We will see this message you've received."

It must have been a text. Yaroslav's forehead creased as he scanned the screen. He handed it to Zoya. "What do you want to do?"

Nash remained still. Thinking.

Phone in hand. What good was the toggle if it still vibrated without it? Technology… he would never understand it all. That was all Milena. Smart. Beautiful.

He'd take her away from all this craziness when it was over.

He swiped his fingers over the number pad. Milena had installed the app on a back page, so it didn't show on the front screen.

Zoya snatched the phone from him before he could touch his text.

She pressed her lips together, a few decades of stress creases gathering around her incongruous red lips.

"Who is Bryon?" She asked.

"I work for him."

Zoya nodded. She looked up at Yaroslav. "No delays. He will not play me the fool."

She smiled at Nash, slow, coyly. "I apologize for the misunderstanding. One cannot be too careful when their husband has gone rogue."

Nash had no clue what that was supposed to mean. It would feel a lot better if Yaroslav would take the gun off him.

Zoya smiled, giving Yaroslav back his phone and holding on to Nash's.

"It appears you've been invited to dine with us." Zoya rose.

"My phone?" Nash hated to ask.

"I think I'll hold on to it until after dinner. Ivan, help Mr. Dunford prepare. I believe we will all see Milena soon."

16

Milena lived in the dark. There was no way they could expect her to go anywhere for dinner. Her father had fussed, and Callahan had promised. Neither of them had ever suffered a migraine like the one Callahan had invoked in her.

While she lay, her eyes closed and unable to face the light, Nash had the Telek. How far would Callahan go to get it?

And her father. She moaned.

He'd used her. Set her up.

And her mother.

She took a deep breath, determined to shake off the pounding in her head.

"Get dressed. Your friend will join us."

Callahan. His voice grated on the last of her nerves. His perky, overconfident smirk made her want to wipe it from his face. She usually never wanted to hurt people. Maybe make him a little uncomfortable for what he'd done to her. According to the Bible, even enemies deserved forgiveness.

She wouldn't quite give him that yet. He hadn't apologized, and she wouldn't ever trust him again, even if her father seemed to approve of the man's methods of running a company and handling his daughter.

Her gut heaved, and the rest of yesterday's shake seemed to gurgle in response. She'd lost any chance of getting away and putting distance between herself and her twisted family.

"Friend?" Had she heard him correctly? Ivan?

His betrayal left a bitterness in her mouth. Arranged marriage or not, she never figured he'd be this low. Or her father would go so far as to create another company to deceive so many people. She got the reason for doing it. She didn't have to agree with it.

"Your boyfriend. The guy from the Shake Shack. Apparently, I won't have to hunt him down after all."

She curled up her legs on the bed. Blinked to focus. She could at least open her eyes now, and the migraine medication had worked its magic to reduce the pain.

"What would you want with him, anyway? You left him there when you took me, remember?"

Callahan made a throaty laugh. "A mistake your father won't let me live down for a while, I'm afraid. Had I known you'd passed off the Telek to him, I would have arranged for him to come with us. But, thankfully, your mother and your betrothed have taken care of that for us. Only know they wish to use him to bargain with us for you."

"For me?" Her father would hold her hostage and use her to get the device they created to bring down his own company and give his new company the edge.

Even with a throbbing headache, she could figure out her father meant to leave Ivan's family with a dying company. But why would Ivan help to destroy a company he would gain when they married? It made little sense.

Milena took a deep breath. In the past couple of days, nothing made sense. She hoped when she woke up, it would have all been a dreadful dream.

It seemed she was still living in it.

"Get dressed, Sleeping Beauty. I picked out your clothes. Make sure you do something to hide those circles under your eyes. They're very unbecoming," Callahan said.

She bit her lip, afraid to let her thoughts spill forth from her tongue. Instead, she recited the Lord's Prayer in her head. *Forgive those who have trespassed against you…*

Callahan stood by the door, his arms crossed, his glasses slid down partway on his nose. In another situation, he might have looked attractive to her. Not the quiet strength of Nash, but from one tech geek to another. But Nash's wide shoulders had always been strong enough to bear her burdens and make her feel safe.

She'd gotten him in this mess.

She owed it to him to get him out.

No matter what it took.

Milena rose off the bed. "Do you need anything else?"

"Just making sure you're dressed and ready to go."

"I'm not very well getting dressed in front of you. Do you mind?" she said, cold, hoping he'd feel the frost and vacate.

Callahan chuckled. "I know how long you ladies like to take to prep yourselves. You've got twenty minutes. Then I'll be back."

He sounded like Arnold Schwarzenegger in *Terminator*: *I'll be back.*

She watched him go and waited for the door to click shut. She hurried to lock it and tried not to scream her frustration as she found the door had no lock from the inside.

Landlines were a thing of the past, and, being the daughter of a tech tycoon, she shouldn't have been surprised to find the phone jack in the wall empty. The house was a new build, which told her that her father's older sensibilities had the builders put in the phone jack.

She shouldn't have pitched her phone, but it was the only way to keep them from tracking her. Nash had the Telek, and she needed to get to him and warn him before they got their hands on him.

She tried not to think of his reaction when he found out her father was behind his. How did she not see this coming?

She went into the bathroom of what must have been a guest room. She needed a shower. She looked like a zombie and moaned like one, too.

Less than an hour later, she stood outside with her father and Callahan waiting for the driver to bring the car around.

Callahan kept his hand on her arm.

"Did you have a good nap?" her father asked.

"My head hurts," she said.

Milo Borghese frowned.

"I'll get you some ibuprofen," Callahan said.

The Rolls pulled up, and she had no choice but to get in and sit between her father and Callahan.

Milena leaned closer to her father.

"You stick with your papa. This is all for the better. You will see. This is a minor bump in the path to our greater success. Your mother thinks she has won, and we will let her. You will put on a pretty smile for Ivan, and he will not be the wiser." Her father's tone, confident she would go along with his plan.

She sat a little straighter, closed her eyes, and gave her eyes more rest. A dull ache plagued the back of her neck and tap-danced on her temples. It made it easy for her to not like Callahan or his methods of getting what he wanted. What happened with Benson had gone over the top.

"The two of you will soon be happily united. How will you ever explain things to the other guy?" Callahan said, sarcasm in his voice.

"I told you I wouldn't marry Ivan."

"I wholeheartedly agree. He is another accessory we don't need," Callahan sat back, smug.

"Enough." Her father's hands balled into a fist. "We stick to the plan."

He reached over, took Milena by the hand. "Your mother leaves me with no choice. You will do as I say, and everything will come out as it should."

For a second, the sincerity in his voice made her believe him.

"Shall we?" Callahan got out and held his hand out for her.

As the car pulled up in front of the Oyster House, her father squeezed her hand. "Please, Mila."

"Just so I understand." Mila licked her lips. She couldn't care less if Callahan's hand fell off waiting for her. She had to get her mind and her heart in check. What if her father was manipulating her? What if her mother wasn't the bad one? Why couldn't she feel which was right?

"Mother gets the money she wants. Ivan gets the company, and you are free of your debt to Yaroslav and can move on with your own company, which you've been letting Callahan run."

Callahan ducked his head into the car, since she hadn't budged to go in his direction.

"And what do you expect of me, Father?" Her voice lowered as she got nauseous.

"You will go in there and do as I have instructed. You will go with Ivan and will bring back the Telek. It is simple. When the time comes, you marry him. I will give your hand as expected. You will be our inside of what goes on in Borghese, and when the time comes, you will leave there and join me again."

"With Callahan still running the business?"

"We shouldn't keep them waiting. Tick. Tock." Callahan tapped his watch.

"Go."

She slid out of the car, her body on autopilot. Outside of the car, holding Callahan's arm, she jumped as the car door shut. Glancing behind her, she watched the car slowly pull away.

"You didn't think he would risk having her see him and blow the deal?" Callahan turned to face her. "Your father talks too much. If you talk and ruin our plans, you'll be floating in the harbor. Understand?"

His eyes glinted, and his features darkened. Milena tried to shake off his hold on her. "Perfectly."

She started toward the door. He reached out and opened it for her first. "In a hurry to see your boyfriend?"

Instantly, Nash popped into her head, but that was wrong. Nash wasn't her boyfriend. Not anymore. And Ivan. Well, she had to get through dinner first. "Ivan? How do you know he'll have the Telek?"

There was no way he could have known she'd given it to Nash.

"Why else would he bring your boyfriend? Won't this be fun?" Callahan grinned.

Milena's heart sank into her stomach.

17

Two men sat at a table, waiting for the others to arrive. Nash's knee shook. Under the table, Ivan kept a gun pointed at the hope of future generations of Dunfords.

Without his phone, he couldn't see if Bryon had texted back. Had Bryon gone to the Borghese house? What would Zoya say and do to him?

The woman had invisible green claws, and while Milena may have inherited her mother's beauty, she'd gotten her brains from her father. Milena was too generous, caring, and good-hearted to have come from such selfish people. Who would use their daughter to pay for their freedom?

Ivan shifted in his seat, and Nash rose at the sight of Milena walking into the dining room. Ivan shoved the gun into his groin, and Nash grunted.

"Where's your manners?" he gritted through his teeth.

Ivan sat back. "Sit and don't say a word."

Milena's hair rippled in waves around her face. She wore a black dress made of thick lace and matching heels.

As she got closer, her eyes widened, her face paler than the last time he'd seen her. Her left eye twitched a little as she put on a smile. "Ivan."

"Are you okay, my darling?" he asked.

"She's fine," the man beside her said. He pulled out a chair and offered for her to sit. Nash recognized the glasses and the man's hair. He wore a plain shirt beneath a sport jacket with jeans and expensive boots.

Milena sat, her eyes meeting his. Pain. She touched her temple, rubbed a moment while the man took his seat beside her.

"I will hear this from my betrothed," Ivan said.

"I'm fine. I feel I may have another migraine coming on." She pulled out the cloth napkin, placed it on her lap as a waiter approached.

"Dinner first, business after?" Callahan asked.

Ivan motioned for the waiter to give them a few more minutes. "I will dine with Milena alone when this is over. We will take care of business now."

"Ivan." Milena's foot came in contact with Nash's leg. It had to be her foot because no one else was wearing high heels at the table. Did she mean to play footsie with him? The thought of her rubbing her foot up Yaroslav's leg sent a spike of jealousy inside him.

"You need to eat. Your head is bothering you. What did you do to her?"

The other guy smirked. He sat back in a chair and placed his hands on the table. "Only what was necessary to secure our deal. Can I assume since you brought a guest, you have your part of the bargain?"

Ivan reached into his jacket pocket and pulled out a cell phone.

Milena frowned.

Nash gave her what he hoped she would take as a sympathetic scowl, if ever there was such a thing.

"Brilliant," the man said. "A phone. And the files?"

"As soon as the payment is secure, Milena will send them. Won't you, darling?"

It made him grit his teeth, but Nash kept a lookout. The dining room area on the second level of the Oyster House was crowded with patrons. The clattering of the silverware and people talking swarmed around them.

"You are still expecting payment?"

Ivan's brows drew together. "We had a deal."

"That was before. Now, you get your precious betrothed back. Unless she is not worth having back?"

Nash moved forward, and Yaroslav glanced over at him. The gun pressed against his thigh.

"What are you doing?" Milena asked.

"Not now," Yaroslav said.

"You don't have the files, do you, Ivan? My father has them," she said.

The man beside her grabbed her arm. "Watch what you say."

Nash tensed. He wanted to fly up over the table and shove the man away from Milena. Out of the corner of his eye, he spotted a guy that looked like Bryon. What was his brother thinking coming here?

"You take this. It has what you want," Ivan said.

"That's mine," Nash said.

"He has no idea, does he? Very clever." The man wagged his finger at Milena.

A waitress came near. Nash recognized her. Jaylene. Bryon shouldn't have gotten her involved. Milena noticed her too. Her frown deepened. She reached up and twirled her finger in her hair. "Give him the phone, Nash. Ivan will buy you another. He'll have plenty of money once Callahan pays him for my hard work. And if he doesn't, I'll see that my father does."

Something had happened in the brief time they'd been apart.

The man beside her shook his head as Jaylene came near with a pitcher of water. She backed off, and Nash caught her glance toward Bryon. What were the two of them planning?

Milena's attitude worried him. She appeared defeated. Deflated. What happened to the determination to keep the device from going to their competitor?

She knew something.

He would have a bruise soon from the point of the gun in his thigh.

"The phone?" the man asked.

Nash played it cool until he could get a suitable read on Milena, so he shrugged. "Take it. I was going to upgrade anyway."

As the man reached for the phone, Yaroslav kept his hand on it. "The money?"

Milena rolled her eyes, sighing loudly.

"No files. No money."

"You have the device." Yaroslav leaned forward, the gunpoint slipping from Nash's leg. He shifted his leg away, scooted closer to Milena.

"Give him the money," Milena said, tossing her cloth napkin on the table. "Give him the device, Ivan. It was never yours to bargain with. Money. No money. I'm done with this. Excuse me, but I'm going to be ill."

Before any of the men could stand, Milena was on her feet. She wavered a little, and Jaylene spotted her.

"Ladies' room?" Milena asked.

Jaylene weaved around a table of five and pointed to the far end of the room.

"Finish your business, Ivan. Then one of you will take me home."

The man who'd brought her rose to his feet. He took her by the elbow. Leaning in, he whispered in her ear. The look of disquiet curled in Nash's gut. Yaroslav didn't like it either. His eyes narrowed.

The poor guy probably didn't realize his gun dangled in his hand. Nash moved, but Yaroslav came to his senses and pointed the gun again. "Sit. Don't move." Then he glanced at Milena. "You will come back, or our guest may not survive until the appetizer."

Milena turned her head, her eye twitching.

Pain laced her expression.

"Don't be dramatic, darling. I'm just going to the ladies' room." She strutted across the room. Jaylene looked up from attending to a table close to him.

The man pulled out an envelope from his pocket, thick and held together with a rubber band. "Half. You'll get the other half when the files are received and confirmed. Take it or leave it."

Nash caught a movement in the corner of his eye. He ignored it, watching as Milena headed out of sight. Another woman, one dressed in black slacks and an emerald green blouse, rose and followed her.

In a blink, the two men exchanged the phone and the envelope. The man standing nodded at Nash. "What about him?"

"You got a problem with me?" Nash asked.

"I have a problem with other people knowing my business," the man said.

"Sorry. I didn't catch your name," Nash said.

The man tugged on his suit jacket. "And you won't."

"He won't be a problem," Yaroslav said, glancing in the direction of the ladies' room.

"You should check on her. She has a habit of disappearing on the way to restrooms." Nash tilted his head, peered in the same direction. He glanced at the standing man, grinned as he spotted Jaylene heading their way.

"You gentleman ready to order?"

Down the hall, Milena leaned against the wall and pressed her fingers to the center of her forehead. A hand grazed her elbow, and she jumped.

"Hey, it's okay," a woman said.

Milena swallowed down the bile rising in her throat. This entire situation made her ill. It took her a moment to recognize Gina. "What happened to your hair?"

"It's called going undercover. Tell me the truth. I'm not playing games. Is Nash in trouble?"

Milena peered around Gina, leaned back against the wall, and whispered, "Yes."

"Tell me what's going down?"

"How did you know we were here?" Milena asked.

"Nash's brother called. I know about the deal and the device."

"If I don't go back to the table soon, Ivan will hurt Nash."

Gina stepped closer to her as a gentleman passed them. "There is no way to get you out of here without passing the table. They have broken no laws. No body, no proof besides your word and Nash's on who shot at you." Gina made a face. "I'm doing this for Nash."

"Of course you are." She moved past Gina, going into the ladies' room. She should at least visit the room since she said she was going there. She didn't want anyone to come looking for her and see her with Gina. Although with that black-haired wig, Gina didn't look at all like Gina.

And Jaylene. Her heart palpitated. What was she doing here?

A part of her got a little elated at having someone else care for her besides her best friend, Alysa. Then again, they were here for Nash. She had to remember they didn't know her.

And all she seemed to do was cause trouble.

Gina reached up and touched her ear. "The man you walked in with?"

"Roland Callahan. He's the CEO of Boyko Technology. He works with my father."

At seeing Gina's surprised face, Milena pinched the bridge of her nose. "Long story. If you want an explanation, it will have to wait until Nash is safe."

"Agreed." Gina stood back and gave Milena space to rip a paper towel from the wall and dampen it with cold water. "Callahan is about to exit the building."

"He's only doing what my father hired him to do. I have to go back, Ivan is edgy. I've never seen him like this before. I think he might have a gun on Nash."

"What makes you think that?"

Her face turned a little flush. Milena dabbed the cool, damp paper towel against the back of her neck. "I felt it." With her foot, when she slid her foot alongside Ivan's. It was something they did at dinner with her parents. Ivan had started it, across the table, a cute game she learned to enjoy at her parents' expense. Until she slipped off her shoe, toed a little too high, and Ivan had lifted his chin. He knew she knew.

She took a deep breath and let it out slowly, her headache threatening to come back more intense than before. She gritted her teeth. She wouldn't forgive her father or Callahan for creating this pain for some time to come.

"We'd better get back. Your fiancé is looking anxious."

Milena didn't question how she knew. The woman was wired, and so was Milena.

"You're coming with me?"

"I'm an old friend. You can introduce me. It will make less of a scene," Gina said.

She headed back to the table with Gina.

She spotted Jaylene, who smiled, and several tables over sat Bryon. Over at the bar stood a broad-shouldered man in a dark button-up shirt with a drink in his hand. Her blood chilled. "Anton."

Gina followed her gaze.

"The man who shot at us," Milena explained, her voice barely audible as she tried to keep a smile plastered on her face.

"I was beginning to worry." Ivan stood, keeping his hand nearest to Nash out of sight. He slid something behind his back. The gun, perhaps? He offered to help Milena with her chair.

"I ran into a friend." Milena waved her hand toward Gina. "Ivan this is—"

"It's nice to see you again, Mr. Yaroslav."

Ivan tensed. His gaze shifted between Milena and Gina. "It appears we have many acquaintances here tonight."

"It must be tonight's special," Gina said and turned her attention to Nash. "I wondered what happened to you. I've been holding our table for the past twenty minutes. You should have called that you got here first."

"My phone is out of order." Nash rose beside Ivan. "I'm sorry I've kept you waiting. If you'll excuse me, I am not one to keep a lady waiting."

"Not so fast." Ivan reached in his pocket, and Milena tensed.

Gina stiffened.

Ivan pulled out several hundred-dollar bills and held them out to Nash. "For your phone. I owe you a replacement."

"What happened to your phone?" Gina asked.

Ivan slid his wallet back. "An accident."

Slowly, Nash took the money.

Gina kept her eyes on Ivan. "I hope you don't mind. I invited Sheila, Rodney, and Bryon to join us." Gina moved to take Nash's arm. She nodded toward Milena. "Enjoy your evening."

Her eyes trailed back to the bar. Milena clutched Ivan, more for the dizzy spell and nausea in her head than having Anton at the bar watching them.

Nash gave her a long hard look. "You should have the lobster and risotto. It's the best."

Milena couldn't say a word. She watched as Gina and Nash moved away from the table. Ivan relaxed the further they moved away. "I believe we should take our dinner to go. Your mother is worried about you."

He tossed a couple of bills on the empty table and escorted her out of the dining room. Anton remained at the bar. Milena gave one last glance at Nash, sitting down with Gina at the table with Bryon.

She was surprised Ivan hadn't said a word about Gina's change in appearance.

Outside, Ivan walked her to a car.

"No driver? I saw Anton. I thought he came with you."

"He did, but he is taking care of other matters for me."

Meaning Nash. She almost asked what he planned to do.

She looked away. The pain returned to the center of her brain. Ivan took her chin, directing her gaze back to him. "You are wondering what just happened. I can see the confusion in your eyes. That arrogant lackey did something to you."

There it was, the concern in his eyes and his voice. Standing with the passenger side door open, he reached and tucked a piece of her hair back from her face. His thumb brushed against her cheek. Yet, she felt nothing. Not the way she had with Nash.

"It's a headache. I'll be fine. I just need to rest."

"I can explain. It's not what you think," Ivan said.

She allowed him to pull her into his arms, to hold her for a moment, her cheek against his shoulder. "I have debts. Back in Russia. I owe people."

Milena pulled back. "You realize you have destroyed my father's company and our future."

"Your father destroyed the company long ago with his betrayal. The other half of the money goes to your mother. She will explain."

He had no idea of the betrayal of her father. "What will happen to Nash?"

Ivan frowned. "Nothing. I have the phone."

She wanted to believe him. "You sent Anton and the man after me. He tried to kill me!"

Ivan's eyes widened. "Kill you? No! I sent Anton to protect you."

She bit her lip against the pain, in her head. "And the other man?"

Ivan gripped her shoulder tighter. "What man? Viktor? Malcolm? I sent them to the airport."

She would get nowhere arguing with him. "Please, Ivan, take me home. I just want to go home." She slid into the passenger seat of the car. He shut the door gently.

Sitting in the driver seat beside her, he paused and looked her over. "Once we marry, I will pay the debts. We will both be free to continue our lives as we wish."

She wanted to believe him. More than anything, she wanted to believe this would all get resolved with vows and a ring. She closed her eyes, ignoring the pain in her head, and the wrongness settling into her heart.

"I don't like taking you home, alone, in this condition. Perhaps to go to your mother's would be best."

"No. I don't want to see my mother right now. I don't want to see anyone. I just want my bed, a dark room, and to rest until my head feels better."

Ivan's jaw muscle twitched. "I'm sure she'll understand."

18

"That was too easy." Bryon hooked his arm around Jaylene.

"I can't believe you called Gina." She would never let him live it down.

Jaylene snuggled in against Bryon, happy to squish between the two brothers. "I don't know. He did have a gun on you. Maybe you need to watch your back for a while."

The first thing he needed to do was get his number switched, get a new phone, and try to contact Milena. She wasn't okay.

She'd been on a race to keep the device from Yaroslav's hands, then was kidnapped, and his mind was still trying to wrap around her giving in. She knew something.

His grip tightened on the wheel. Yaroslav owed him for more than a phone. He had bullet holes in the side of his truck.

Gina couldn't hold them on anything. She could question Anton about his truck, but he didn't want that trouble coming back around.

He wanted Milena. Safe. With him.

Pulling up in front of his house, he let Bryon and Jaylene out.

"You coming?" Bryon held his door open for Jaylene to slide out.

"I think I should stay somewhere else tonight. In case they come around."

He figured Bryon would argue with him. Jaylene got back in the truck. "You can drop me off at my place. It's getting late anyhow."

"I'll take you home. I don't want you in any more dangerous situations," Bryon said.

Jaylene turned, smacked Bryon on the cheek, and quipped, "Sure thing, babe."

Was Milena okay?

All he seemed to do was worry about her lately.

Something still didn't sit right in his gut.

"I'll call you as soon as I get a phone." Probably not until morning.

"Don't forget, we have that job we need to start tomorrow near the harbor."

He remembered, and he needed to swing by Oliver and Shirley's place to thank them for helping him.

Bryon tapped on the dash to get his attention.

"Don't spend all night watching and waiting for her to come home. You heard what Gina said. No crime. I know you care about her, but you don't need to be caught up in any more family business with that one. And take this if you need it." Bryon slid a handgun onto the seat. His gun.

Nash took it and put it back in the dash where he could find it.

An hour later, he sat outside Milena's place. No lights.

Had Yaroslav taken her to her parents' place?

He turned on some music, nothing loud. He needed to

soothe his nerves and let his brain rest from the whirlwind he'd been in the past few days.

He waited for a car, for lights. Anything to signal Milena had returned.

If not, in the morning he'd go stake out her parents' place. He wouldn't attempt to go inside again. His thigh had a bruise the size of a baseball thanks to Yaroslav's gunpoint. What had that been all about?

He rubbed his face.

He asked himself why he couldn't walk away this time. Guilt. Maybe?

Gina had put her neck out there for him tonight. He would thank her later. Nothing a friend wouldn't do for a friend.

One day, some lucky guy would dance on the moon to have a girl like Gina. Brave. Believer. Best Friend.

But he'd given his heart to Milena.

Somehow she'd have to accept it. He couldn't let her marry Yaroslav.

Exactly what kind of blackmail had the man used?

———

"Your dress fitting is at two o'clock."

Zoya Borghese refused to take no for an answer.

Milena spent almost a week avoiding both her parents, Nash, and keeping in the dark. She wouldn't have even gotten out of bed if Zoya hadn't pounded down the door and threatened to call the cops.

Tempted to tell her mother to call them, Milena winced at the idea of having to deal with Gina again. As if the woman needed one more excuse not to like her.

Ivan had brought her a new phone.

She had spent hours in the early morning the day before taking it apart and removing the tracking chip and reprogramming it before she decided she would use it.

He brought her food and offered to stay inside with her in the evenings to watch her favorite romantic comedy movies. She could tell it took him a lot of effort to do so, but she wasn't about to let him off the hook that easily.

There were things she knew. Things she wished she didn't.

Her parents were waiting for her wedding before they divorced.

She could see the gleam in Zoya's eyes as she tried to manipulate Milena into making the last decisions for the wedding. They had moved the date up to the end of the month. How convenient. Milena reluctantly gave in.

She stood inside a bridal shop while her mother made selections of dresses for her.

"Don't you wish to look at them or pick a few?" the salesclerk, a slender, dark-skinned woman with long braids, asked.

"Let my mother choose. It pleases her."

Milena had called her friend Alysa. Repulsed by what had happened, she'd stayed up all night on her revamped phone and drunk a bottle of wine she'd received as an early wedding gift. Normally, she didn't drink.

A girl deserved a night of self-pity.

She paid for it in the morning. The buzz in her head told her she wouldn't do it again.

At the sight of her standing in front of a wall of mirrors wearing a mermaid-style dress, Milena's mother dabbed the tears in her eyes. Milena turned to the side, and everything inside her said this was the dress.

She imagined Nash standing at the front of the church. Instantly, her bliss popped like a bubble. Ivan, not Nash.

She couldn't marry him.

When the salesclerk found her the perfect veil, Milena refused to try on any more dresses.

"But it's just the first one."

"I know the right one when I see it." And this was it.

Milena's mother did not object. She wanted to go out to lunch and afterward taste cake samples.

Ivan had promised to meet them for the cake tasting, but first he had business to attend to at the office—business that should have been dealt with by her and her father.

A low burn spread through her stomach.

Ivan had promised to explain. He had debts.

What did that mean?

Throughout lunch with her mother, Milena picked at her salad. She hadn't seen Nash since the evening at the restaurant. She couldn't exactly go running to him, could she?

"All this business with your father and that evil man giving you a headache has dampened what should have been the happiest moment of your life." Zoya patted her lips with her napkin.

What Milena wouldn't give for carb-filled pasta and the scents of Momma Shirley s.

She hadn't expected that, nor had she expected her life to spin out of control as it did. How many times had she tried to call Nash, only to remember he no longer had a phone and the number would most likely result in Callahan answering?

"I'm not happy. You're right, Mother." Milena shoved her salad away.

"You must not blame Ivan. This is your father's fault. It

would serve him good to have that other company put him out of business."

Her mother didn't know.

"And what of the debt? Do you think Ivan's family wants to gain control of a business that is failing?"

Zoya waved a hand. "It won't fail. Not with you taking over in your father's place. Ivan may have a head for business, but you are an engineer like your father. It would serve him right for what he's done."

"And what has he done?"

He sold the secrets of his own company. Not to mention, he tried to use company resources and his daughter to pay off an old debt.

Her heart fell. Of all the people, she never expected her father would do something this deceptive. And her mother…

Zoya sat back, picking up her water glass, looking down her nose at Milena. "Traitor." She hissed. "I was the one who got him out of Russia. I made the deal that saved his skin, and this is where he left me." She spread her arms and scowled.

Milena was seeing a new side of her mother, betrayal, hurt, and something much deeper. Revenge flashed in the woman's eyes, deadly and dark.

"I want no part of this." Milena scooted back and picked up her purse.

Zoya put down her drink and frowned. "I know, my dear. Ivan feels terrible about what has happened. But you have your entire married life for him to make it up to you. Let us hope he is better at being appreciative than your father was."

Milena bit her lip against saying all the things that came to mind. Her father had sold out his own company and his daughter to pay off a debt, while his greed had caused him to betray his wife, and for what? Money? Reputation?

All the things her parents had raised her to avoid.

"We still have time before the tasting. I think I would like to swing by the church, and I'll meet you there."

"Confessions can wait for later. Come, some cake will make you feel better. We should not keep your groom waiting, shall we?"

―――――

Shirley and Oliver hosted the next weekly lunch at their place. Shirley still hummed in the kitchen, putting together plates of her latest creation. Nash could smell the jalapeno in the sauce. Sean took a seat beside him. The grim expression on Gina's face as she arrived made him wince.

She took a seat between him and Oliver.

"What's up, buttercup?" Oliver leaned into her, shoulder to shoulder. "You look like you have had a rough night. This guy causing you trouble again?"

Gina snorted. "I thought we ended the drama a few days ago."

She hadn't looked at him. Sean poured her a cup of coffee and slid it in her direction. Tina and Rae walked through the door. The little bell rang, and Shirley called a greeting from back in the kitchen. For once, they were all together in their circle.

"What trouble?" Tina asked as she sat down next to Sean and Rae sat next to Tina.

"Boy here got back involved with an old flame. Went for quite a chase, too," Sean said. "Broke my coffee table."

Nash groaned. "I'll buy you a new one."

"We had calls of suspicious activity outside the condos near Inner Harbor," Gina said.

"And that's what put circles under your eyes?" Sean took over, making sure everyone had a good dose of coffee to get their circle going.

After last week's run with Milena, he figured this would be a topic of discussion before they got into their usual Bible study material and catching up with each other's lives. Milena would be a hot topic for a while. One he couldn't seem to press into a place and forget anymore.

"You've been staking out her place," Nash said.

"And so have you." Gina took a long, drawn-out gulp of her coffee. She smiled and gave Sean an appreciative look. He must have made her coffee just right.

"I need to leave the circle early today, guys. Police business. And Nash"—she turned her head to look at him—"I need you to come down to the station with me."

"Oh Nash, what did you do now?" Tina teased.

A hairdresser from the east side, Tina always had her hair in some new updo. Today it was curled and hung in ringlets at the back of her head.

"I hate to be the killjoy of our circle today," Gina said. "But we found a dead body in the harbor last night."

"Don't you guys find dead bodies in the harbor all the time?" Sean asked.

"Do you know who it was?" Rae asked.

A housewife from a few streets over, Rae didn't get out much and, beyond the weather, refused to read or watch the news. Life was depressing enough, she'd told them. Their circle was her weekly getaway while a neighbor kept an eye on the kids so she could have a coffee break.

"African-American male. Fits the description of a man who went missing last week and believed murdered."

"You think it could be the driver who works for Borghese?"

"Does this have anything to do with that article in the paper? The one about Borghese Technology and Boyko Technology trading secrets or something like that?"

"Something like that." Gina said.

Nash hadn't read the article. He had done little for the past several days beyond helping Bryon on their next job and sitting outside of Milena's house at night. Relief had washed over him to finally see the lights on inside her place.

How many times had he wanted to go inside and talk to her?

By now, she would have gotten a new phone, as he had. Neither of them had each other's numbers.

"It's quite the scandal here in town," Tina said. "I heard it from one of the ladies in the shop talking about it. Old money, divorce, and plain old greed."

While Tina shook her head, Sean gave him an apologetic look.

"Wow. Does this got anything to do with that hottie you brought into my place that was in trouble?" Oliver asked.

His friends knew more than he did at this point.

Oliver was just lucky Shirley was still in the kitchen. Gina reached over and punched him in the arm on Shirley's behalf.

"You identified the body?" Nash asked.

Gina leaned back, her hands cupped around the coffee cup. "I can't go into details. The case is still open, but we believe we may have a prime suspect."

"It was the girl, wasn't it?" Tina asked, too much enthusiasm in her voice for Nash's liking.

But Milena wouldn't have done something like this. She'd been home all night. He'd sat in his truck and been sure of it. She wouldn't hurt a living soul. He needed to talk to her.

"Perhaps." Gina wouldn't say much. She couldn't.

"But she's on your list," Nash asked.

Shirley came out with a large bowl of pasta. Plates were already on the table. "Who'd like some of my hot bowtie pasta?"

No one said anything. They all looked at Gina, waiting for her to answer.

Nash hadn't realized he held his breath until his lungs demanded air, and slowly, he breathed as Gina said, "She's getting ready to skip town. I warned her it wouldn't be wise during a police investigation. Under the circumstances, I can't blame her."

Nash's brows furrowed together. "What do you mean, she's skipping town?"

Gina shrugged. "She claimed she was packing for her honeymoon. I warned her about leaving town until we resolve this."

She'd wanted him to take her to the airport when she'd come running to him. Where would she go? A friend. Was she trying to get out of marrying Ivan?

Maybe he had a chance.

"Ew…" Rae shivered. "Can we talk about something else? I don't want to go home to my babies with that scary stuff in my head all day. It's bad enough horrid things happen to people every day. I'd rather not have it imprinted on me to be afraid when I go home."

Rae had anxiety issues. It was one of the reasons her husband, Trey, had encouraged her to join a circle at church and tried to get her into playgroups with the children. She felt safer at home and rarely ventured anywhere that wasn't essential.

"Sure. Nash and I need to discuss some things that happened, and Sean, you too, as I understand they were at your place. That's all I can say at this point."

And it left Nash with more questions.

His first priority was Milena.

"I need to go."

They all looked at him as if he'd suddenly grown three heads.

"See, this kind of stuff should stay out of the circle. We need to talk about positive things," Rae said. "My little Mannie took three steps yesterday!"

Sean grinned at her.

"You'll all need to try my new recipe. I've been working on it all morning," Shirley said.

So they ate, and Nash took off shortly after they finished their circle with prayer. He drove straight to Milena's place, banged on the door, and no one answered.

He texted Bryon to say he would be late getting back. The other guys on the crew could help handle the cleanup.

Spotting a neighbor, Nash inquired about Milena.

No one had seen her.

19

Milena had tasted enough cake that if she never saw another piece in her lifetime, it would be all right with her.

They were several samples into the cake tasting when Anton appeared in the shop. Her mother had declared the white chocolate with raspberry to be the best of them, and Milena hadn't disagreed.

With no other choice than to start without Ivan, Milena allowed her mother to decide about the flavor and design. Her heart wasn't in it, but it distracted Zoya from Milena's father and her train of complaints against the man.

While Zoya discussed designs with the cake artist, Anton, Ivan's right-hand man and bodyguard, appeared in the shop.

"Mr. Yaroslav apologizes for his absence. He wishes me to take you to him as he has been delayed by other business."

"Go. Go." Zoya shooed her away. "I will finish up here. You and Ivan can take care of the meeting with the priest, and I will see you for dinner."

Anton held the door for her to leave the shop.

Milena shook her head. Was her mother crazy? Oh, yes, she forgot. Her mother didn't know. Milena tried to think of an excuse. "I think it is best I finish up here with the cake and then go over to the church. I would not want Ivan's and my day to become delayed because of business."

A business that made her unable to sleep at night and packed and ready to flee as soon as she was able.

"Go. Ivan wants you to be with him. I will take care of this."

Anton waited. Patiently. It unnerved her. "I don't think that would be a good idea. If Ivan wishes to see me, he can come when he is free. I'm sure Anton has better things to do on company time than chauffeur me."

Her fingers felt icy, and she rubbed them together to bring the heat back to the tips.

Zoya asked the baker to wait a moment. He was a portly man, with a shiny spot atop his head and a smile as big as Broadway at a price, because Zoya was willing to pay for a cake for her daughter's wedding.

Milena should have lied and said her head still hurt enough to stay home and then waited until she could escape. Running, however, hadn't gotten her anywhere.

Nor did she have any intentions of going with Anton.

The man had chased and shot at her!

She'd have to tell her mother. Just one more thing on the list of reasons for her mother to hate her father. They were adults. They would have to deal with it.

And Milena would have to accept that neither of her parents were the people she'd envisioned them as being. Her father had contacted her twice. Her mother always worried about the wedding proceeding. She reminded him of the deal, the money. Ivan's debt. Her mother's share.

The files. The device she and her father created. Together.

No one thought of her.

Except maybe Nash.

What had her father done to him this time? Not that she blamed him. She'd stay far, far away from him herself, rather than get caught up in this drama and danger.

Anton cleared his throat. "I assure you, Ms. Borghese, it is no trouble. Mr. Yaroslav sent me to ensure your safety."

She tried not to snort at this.

"See. You are safe," Zoya said.

Milena pulled her mother aside, lowered her voice, and said, "He was with the man who shot at Nash and me in the parking garage. I can't go with him."

Zoya patted her daughter's hand, not at all fazed by what she'd said. "Anton works for Ivan and his family. If he was shooting, it was a scare tactic to protect you from that awful ex-security guard."

Zoya touched her face. She glanced over at the waiting baker and then at Anton before returning her gaze, filled with compassion, toward Milena. "I know it scares you. If Anton makes you feel uncomfortable, you will talk to Ivan about it. He trusts Anton with his life, and with yours. Go. Talk to Ivan. Soon, the two of you will marry, and I can only hope it is a better match than your father and I were."

She could see she wouldn't get anywhere with her mother. A glint of determination flicked in Zoya's gaze, and in the pat of her hand, and before Milena could protest further, her mother stretched out her hand and placed it on Anton's arm.

"I will call and catch up with you later."

As soon as they were outside, Milena took her hand from Anton's arm. "Is Ivan at the office?"

Anton nodded.

"I need to stop by the church first. You can go ahead and tell him I'll be there shortly."

Anton's eyes narrowed. "My instructions are to bring you to Mr. Yaroslav."

"I'm not getting in a car with you, and if you try to force me, I'll scream," she said.

Anton smiled. "You will get in the car. You will go with me to see Ivan, and once our business is settled, I will take you anywhere you want to go."

Anton's slip in protocol caused Milena's heart to stutter. "Ivan isn't at the office in Borghese Technology is he?"

Anton took her by the arm, yanked her to keep walking with him, heading to the black Rolls Royce parked a few cars ahead on the street. "He is waiting for you in your father's old office."

"He's taking over," she muttered.

As they approached the car, Milena noticed there was no one else in it. Where was the other guy? Ivan had two men working with him. Anton and, for the life of her, she couldn't think of the others' names. Viktor and Nik, maybe?

She hadn't seen the other guy since the parking garage.

"Where's your partner?" she asked. "I figured he would wait for us in the car."

"He has been indisposed. Get in. We're wasting time."

Anton unlocked the car, wrenched open the door, and Milena tried to pull away, but Anton shoved her down into the seat. He held her, clipping on her seat belt, his face in her face, and Milena froze.

Fear coiled down her spine. "We don't want to keep Mr. Yaroslav waiting."

The door slammed shut. Milena grabbed the handle.

Locked. She tried to reach for the lock, but someone had removed them from the door. She stretched across to the other side. Gone there too. She held onto the seat belt. Her heart hammered in her chest.

Anton slid into the driver's seat. His eyes met hers from the rearview mirror. He smirked. "Mr. Yaroslav will be happy to see you."

Milena sat back, silently praying nothing bad had happened to Ivan. As much as she didn't want to marry the man, she had a grim feeling. A horrible feeling.

Thankfully, Nash was safe. She reached up, feeling the little cross pendant around her throat.

Because whatever reason Ivan had wanted her to come to the office couldn't be good, she'd been avoiding going in to work for as long as she could. By now, he had to know her father had the files, especially since an anonymous source had tipped off the press and leaked the story of Borghese and Boyko's affiliation.

Her mother had fumed for hours and blamed it on her father wanting attention for his new business. Then she'd calmed down, acted as if it didn't matter, and poured more attention into details of a wedding that shouldn't be happening.

Perhaps now Ivan would listen to her.

Dread, rather than anticipation, knotted inside her.

As Anton drove, Milena prayed.

There had to be a way out of this. All of this.

Ivan sat in her father's old chair, in his old office, and waited.

His hands were tied at the wrist to the chair, and his

eyes bloodshot. Instead of glancing at her, he avoided her gaze.

That grim feeling Milena had before skyrocketed. Everything inside her screamed to turn and run, but Anton stood between her and the door.

"Where is Diane?" She hadn't seen her father's secretary when she came in.

"Ivan sent her out on errands," Anton said.

Nothing to see here. Just an average day at the office. Without her father. With Milena escorted by Anton and Ivan tied to a chair. None of this would appear suspicious. Milena stepped further into the office.

Behind her, the door shut.

She tried not to flinch. Going over to Ivan, she crouched in front of him. Put her hand on his chin and tilted up his gaze.

"I'm sorry," Ivan whispered. "You were never to be a part of this."

"What is the meaning of this?" She turned and confronted Anton. He pulled out a gun, cocked it, and made a show of the sleek handgun.

Anton pointed it at Ivan. "Money. What else?"

"Ivan?"

"He just wants the money, Milena. He'll kill me if your father doesn't pay." Ivan had a gash near his temple. Dried blood stained his white shirt.

"My father didn't send the money for the files?" Of course he wouldn't. Why pay for something he already had? "He could have paid it to Mother directly."

He wouldn't have. Not her father. Not Callahan. They were after building a new tech empire and using her design to launch their success. She stared up at Anton. The gun held steady at Ivan's head.

"This has nothing to do with your mother." Ivan met her eyes.

"Call your father. The money," Anton said.

"What's going on?" She put her hands on Ivan's knees to steady her.

"Please, Milena. Call your father."

"You have a phone. Use it." Anton moved closer, his face grim.

"How much money are we talking about?" Her mind raced to come up with scenarios where they all walked away with no harm.

"How much is your family's company worth?" Anton jerked the gun. He wanted her to grab her phone and make the call.

"You mean *Ivan's* company once we're married." She tried to buy them some time. Would her father answer the phone if she called this time of day? Anton wasn't asking for some small change. Borghese Technology netted in the millions range.

The deal at the restaurant had only been petty cash.

Anton chuckled darkly. "You tell her."

"Tell me what?" Milena froze.

Anton took another step closer, the gun inches from the back of Ivan's head.

What would Nash do in this same situation? Probably take Anton down with a single leap where he'd knock the gun from Anton's hand, and she'd grab it to save them all. Her heart pinched against her ribs.

She wasn't that kind of brave.

And maybe Nash wasn't at all the coward she'd deemed him back in the restaurant when he handed over the phone and her family's future. Her future. Their future.

"I'm not the man you think I am," Ivan said, his voice so soft she almost hadn't heard him.

Milena inched her hand up slowly. She covered his wrist where the zip ties held him to the chair, the desk too far away to grab something sharp to free him. Marks had formed on his skin from the bands.

"I've made some poor investments over the past year," Ivan said.

"He's a thief, like your father." Anton pulled back his shoulders, looking down his nose at them both.

Milena stiffened. "You've been selling our trade secrets to cover your poor investments. And my mother? She knew."

"Yes," Ivan hissed through clenched teeth.

"You will call your father. He will pay up or else," Anton insisted.

Ivan glared up at Anton. He focused again on Milena. "Please, Mila, darling. Call your father. I need the five million dollars, or Anton will kill us both."

She opened her mouth, not sure what to say to this, when suddenly she asked Anton, "What do you get out of this?"

Anton smiled slowly. "I want what is due to me."

"You owe him money."

"I had no choice."

Anton snorted.

It became harder to breathe. "How much? How much does he owe you?"

Anton shrugged. "I will take all I can get. With interest."

Breathe. She could rebuild what she'd lost. Walk away from all this. She wasn't sure exactly how, as now wasn't exactly the best time to try to be a MacGyver.

"We are wasting time. Call. Now."

"You're worse than both our fathers." She went on her knees to ease the ache in her feet from crouching.

"No." Ivan swore in Russian. "I mean, it was. What do you expect? This whole thing has been arranged for decades. You. Me. The company takeover. All my life I am told what I am to do. What was I to get out of it? I made those investments to cut old ties. A fresh start. For us both."

Milena blinked.

Really? Because it felt like she'd gotten played by too many people lately.

She reached for her phone slowly.

Anton lifted his chin, watching her every move.

"I'm calling my father."

Relief sagged in Ivan's shoulders.

With every press of a number on her phone, her heart ricocheted up another notch of panic.

"Speakerphone. So I can hear you," Anton said.

She did as he asked. With each ring of the phone, her chest grew heavier, and it got harder to breathe.

Her father answered. "Mila? Is that you?"

Anton grabbed the phone. "If you want your daughter back alive, Borghese, you'll deliver the files. I want my money."

"Who is this? What is this about?" her father demanded.

"Father?" Milena asked.

"Mila." Another lengthy pause. "Are you okay? Has he hurt you?"

"I'm okay." She raised her voice for the speakerphone. "But Ivan is tied up, and Anton has a gun on us both."

Her father muttered something in Russian, and as his voice rose, he spoke in his native tongue. He threatened

Anton. He didn't care what happened to Ivan, but harm one hair on Milena's head and Milo Borghese would hunt him down.

It would cost him five million dollars.

"You got your money," her father insisted.

"The partial payment is not enough. You complete the deal. The money or you don't see your daughter again."

"What deal?"

Yes, her father would play dumb.

"You will send the man with the money here to your office and leave it with your secretary. If it isn't all here by five o'clock, you'll find your precious daughter floating in the harbor."

Anton ripped the phone from her hand. He turned it off and tossed it on the desk.

"Now, what shall we do while we wait?"

Milena sat back on her butt, leaning against Ivan's legs. His wrist strapped to the arms of the chair, he managed to stretch his fingers far enough to caressed her shoulder. She scooted away, brought up her knees, and laid her head upon them. *Think. Breathe.*

Moments ago, she was letting her mother plan her wedding to Ivan.

"He'll get the money. He won't want anything to happen to you," Ivan said.

She wanted to believe him, reaching up and toying with the pendant around her neck. If ever there was a time for confessions, it was now.

20

Nash wished he'd done things differently, but he couldn't go back and change the past. Milena coming to him after all this time had been a sign. They'd been given a chance to clean the slate, and he'd be a fool to ignore this opportunity.

Nash sat in his truck, watching the minutes tick by on the clock above his radio.

There was no sense in thinking of all the things he could have done but didn't. The fact that Milena trusted him, had faith in him enough to come to him, still resonated deep down.

He had one last chance to protect her. He wanted to tell her what had been lingering in the back of his mind for a long time. He wouldn't let it go. He wouldn't let *her* go.

Where was she?

No one had seen her.

He checked his phone for any new messages. This phone had several new apps and features beyond his last one. He could check his email and order takeout from a touch of his finger. Neither of those would help him.

It rang, and Gina's face appeared under her number. He answered with a "Hello?"

"Viktor Horvath. Age twenty-seven. Employed by Borghese Technology Security. Ring any bells?"

Nash shifted the weight of his stance. "Not a one. I take it this is the dead guy?"

"I wish you would have come down to the station. I don't like talking about this on the phone, and Momma Shirley's wasn't the place."

"You think this was Milena's driver?" Nash stared out at the black-painted door on Milena's condo, willing her to open it or come home.

"The man's neck was broken. Clean. Professional."

"Not Yaroslav."

"Maybe, but I don't think so. He was last seen with another man. Anton Godec. Both men work under Borghese's payroll, but I have a feeling they came with Yaroslav."

"They weren't there when I was there." Convenient, Yaroslav had come right when Milena's father had canned him.

"Good to know. I have sources saying that Yaroslav is deeply in debt, and his investors are looking to collect."

"Explains why he'd sell out trade secrets from a company he was about to own."

It was well past the lunch hour. Where would Milena be? At the office? Retrieving the files? Working on a recent update or some new gadget? She was too smart for her own good. He admired the way her brain worked, even when it made her flighty.

"Someone from the department will head to Borghese Technology to question Yaroslav. It's now a homicide investigation. I wanted to say I was sorry. I let my feelings get in the way, which is why I'm handing this case over to another detective, and they'll be taking it from here."

Nash sat in silence for the next few moments.

Hearing Gina sigh, he spoke up before she hung up.

"I know that was hard for you. I appreciate you sharing this information with me." He sounded like a royal jerk, too formal, and not at all the friend he should be.

Nash cleared his throat to try again. "This has made me have to think and process a lot of things in my life lately."

And she stopped him right there. "Don't go getting sappy on me, Dunsford. I'm doing my job, and like you, I protect those I care about."

He cared about her, too, as a friend. He wouldn't embarrass her anymore or cause her more distress by poking the tenderness of her admission. "And a fine job you do, Detective Fullerton"

"Flattery will get you nowhere," she said.

Gina couldn't see it, but Nash smiled.

"The new detective will want to question Milena. You might want to give her a heads-up and keep an extra eye on her until this case is closed."

Leaving his phone out on the truck seat beside him, Nash headed to the next best place he could think of to find Milena.

Over a half hour later, Nash pulled into the parking lot at Borghese Technology and made his way to the front entrance. He politely avoided the front desk secretary as she answered the phone and juggled signing for a package from the delivery guy at the counter. Nash knew his way around and headed to Milena's office inside the engineering labs toward the back of the building.

Everything appeared peaceful. Men and women were working in cubicles and bent over computers as they wrote what Nash figured were new programs for new upgrades or new prototypes of devices.

He came to Milena's area. No more prestigious than the rest of her coworkers. She had an inspirational quote desk calendar and a stuffed dog in the corner. He'd given that to her one night after they'd walked a street fair. She wouldn't let him get her an actual dog, so he settled on the stuffed one.

The fact she kept it meant something.

A man staring at his iPad as he walked past halted a moment. He glanced at Nash. "Can I help you?"

"I'm looking for Miss Borghese."

The man nodded, glanced back at his iPad. "She's taken the next two weeks off. Something about getting prepared for her wedding. Is there something you need that perhaps I can assist you with?"

Nash shook his head. "I'm a friend of the family and was in town. Thought I'd look her up and see how she's been doing."

"Well"—the man pushed up his glasses—"as you can see, she's not here. You can leave a message with the secretary out front if you wish. I'm surprised she didn't inform you then."

Yeah, well, Nash hadn't stopped to ask. He watched the man walk away.

Milena taking time off did not surprise him. He hoped she had recovered from the caffeine-induced migraine. He wanted to hunt down the guy who had his phone and teach him a lesson on how to treat others, but he had more important things to do.

Milena could be a hundred places.

Why was she still planning on going through with the wedding?

He headed for Yaroslav's office. This blackmail would end, and maybe, just maybe, he could stop Milena from having to go through with marriage to a guy like Yaroslav.

With Milena's father out of town, he would have to rely on the secretary to direct him.

"Mr. Yaroslav has moved into Mr. Borghese's office while he is away."

Already Yaroslav had moved to take over.

Not much to take over if the man kept selling out the company. Was that part of the blackmail? Having Borghese sell out to Boyko? It made sense. Milo Borghese leaving town, the company going to Yaroslav, and the shady side deals. Would he come back for the wedding?

Something wasn't adding up.

He found the desk empty and heard an angry voice on the other side of the door.

How soon before the detective showed up to question Yaroslav or the employees?

Gina giving him the heads-up made him think it would happen soon.

She deserved a guy who could meet her on her turf, talk shop with her after an interminable day of work. They'd always gotten along that way. He'd listened and understood, with a background in security. He'd gone so far as to clean her guns, and she'd sparred with him on the weekends.

Nothing romantic ever came out of her slamming him down on the mat or him disarming her to practice.

His arms flexed, wishing they were around Milena. He pulled back his shoulders and faced Yaroslav.

The door flew open, and Nash stepped in. Sitting on the other side of the desk, Ivan Yaroslav lifted his face, and his eyes widened. "You need to get out. Now."

"I need a word with you."

Ivan rolled his eyes.

"Nash?"

The door shut, and the man from the parking garage stood with a gun pointed at Ivan.

Slowly, Milena rose and came into view.

Nash stared at the man holding the gun. Anton, Yaroslav's right-hand man. Surprised, and somehow not.

"Where is the money?" the man demanded.

"My father sent you?" Milena's hopeful look sent chills to his bones.

Anton pointed the gun at Nash. He held out his hand. "Give it to me now."

Rage swept through Nash, and he tried to swallow it down. He envisioned running through sprinklers in the front yard when he was a kid with his little brother Bryon. He had plans to hold Milena in his arms again. And he was getting sick and tired of this game and all the blackmail. His grandfather would hand him a shovel to get them out of this horse-dung of a situation.

"I can't. I don't have it."

———

Anton's eyes narrowed. "If you don't have the money, why are you here?"

Milena stood in front of Ivan. He pushed her leg with his foot. "Get behind me," he whispered.

She moved behind the chair.

"To assure Mr. Borghese his daughter is safe. For he knows you could dump her and her fiancé in the harbor, and we wouldn't find them floating until a few days later."

Milena paled. What was Nash doing?

He lowered his hands. "You want your money? I just

need to make a call. Mr. Borghese is waiting for me to confirm his daughter is unharmed."

She found it hard to believe her father sent Nash. He knew nothing of her father's involvement, or did he? Nash could read the papers as well as anyone else.

"None of us are getting out of here alive," Ivan said.

"Shut up," Anton snapped at him. He twisted the gun in Ivan's direction.

Nodding toward Nash, he said, "Make the call if you must. You have an hour left."

Don't be a hero, Nash, she silently pleaded.

Nash reached in his pocket. She half expected him to pull out his gun. Instead, he showed Anton the phone.

A buzz came in on the intercom on the phone on the desk. "Mr. Yaroslav. A delivery is here for you. Should I have it sent up?"

Milena gasped.

Anton tensed and Nash dove at Anton.

The gun went off, and Milena hit the floor. She clung to the chair and crawled around the side of Ivan. On the floor, Nash wrestled with Anton.

"Intercom the front desk. Hurry," Ivan said, his voice gritted with pain.

Milena scrambled to grab the phone. She pulled it down on the floor beside her. "Shauna! Call 9-1-1. Anton has Ivan tied up, and he's got a gun. Hurry!"

"Are you sure?"

"Yes!" Milena screamed. The gun went off again, and she felt Ivan jerk in the chair above her. She glanced up, red blossoming his side and staining his shirt.

"Was that gunfire?" Shauna's voice rose to hysterics. "I'm calling 9-1-1!"

Milena moved over to Ivan, his face contorted in pain.

On the other side of him, Nash slammed Anton's hand against the back bookcase, and the gun flew free. It slid and skidded across the floor.

"Get it," Ivan said between clenched teeth.

Milena leaped for the gun, laying across the floor as Anton flipped over on Nash, pulling back his arm to smash his fist into Nash's face.

"Stop, or I'll shoot!" She clutched the gun, aimed it at Anton. Her heart pressed against her lungs and made it hard to breathe. Her hands shook as Anton turned his head, stared at the gun, and froze.

Nash shoved the man off him. "Milena, give me the gun."

Milena sat up, keeping her eyes and the gun focused on Anton. "Ivan's been shot."

It choked her up. Her lip trembled.

She brought herself up to her knees, wobbling as they were, and allowed Nash to come closer.

"I mean it," she warned, as Anton got his legs back under him again.

Nash moved beside her. "You have to cock it like this." He took his fingers over hers and cocked the gun so it would fire again. She trembled.

"I've got this, Mila. Use my phone and call the police. Look after Ivan."

She tried to force her hands to release the gun and couldn't.

"Where is your gun?"

"Milena," Ivan said from behind her.

"He's bleeding."

"Take care of him," Nash said.

She willed her grip to ease and gave the gun over to Nash.

He rose and stood over Anton. "Move, and I can't promise this won't accidentally go off before the police get here."

Milena searched the desk, finding a pair of scissors. Hurriedly, she cut Ivan's ties. He groaned, his hand going to cover his wound.

"I hear sirens," Nash said.

Milena went to leave, to direct them to Ivan sooner. He covered her hand with his cold one. "Milena."

"It's going to be okay, Ivan. Help is coming."

"The money—" But he slumped forward, his chin going to his chest.

"Ivan?" She checked his pulse.

"Serves him right," Anton said.

Nash grunted. "Tell me he just passed out."

"I can't find a pulse!" She panicked.

Anton snorted.

Nash backed over closer to her. He felt for a pulse in Ivan's neck. "There. We need to keep pressure on the wound."

Diane, her father's secretary, came bursting in the door. Her short salt-and-pepper hair curled around her chin. "What on earth is going on in here?"

21

An ambulance and several police cars surrounded the building. Officer Brumel took their prisoner off Nash's hands, cuffing him and shoving him into a car.

EMTs got Ivan onto a stretcher and hoisted him up into the ambulance, headed to the hospital. Nash stayed close to Milena. She went with several officers and made sure all the other employees had cleared out of the building before locking up.

Shauna, the front desk secretary, lingered, and Milena assured her Mr. Yaroslav would survive. Milena needed to go to the hospital, too.

On the front desk, a package had been delivered. Two-point five million dollars with a promissory note from her father for the rest. The banks needed time for that kind of cash. The police took it for evidence.

Too shaken up by the events that had taken place in the building, Diane quit.

Milena had her suspicions she'd soon see Diane working over at Boyko Technology.

Hours later, Milena sat in the waiting room at the hospital, awaiting word on Ivan.

"No, Mother. As soon as I know." Milena allowed the tears to drip down her face.

"They have arrested your father. They won't be able to keep him. As soon as the wedding is over, we're going back to Sortavala. Ivan can come back with us. I'm sure Ruslan won't mind having his son and the company closer in hand."

"There will not be a wedding, Mother. As soon as Ivan is out of the hospital, he'll go straight to jail. Stealing is a crime. I would worry more if he mentioned your name and brought you into this."

"Me?" Her mother laughed. "He has nothing on me. Besides, your father would never press charges for stealing. He stole from himself."

"I wouldn't count on it, Mother. And this time, those files and the device were my design."

Her mother gasped. "Milena Borghese!"

In the background, Milena heard the door, and her mother huffed. "What manner of a child would disgrace their parents?"

Her mother never got to finish her lecture. Milena heard a woman's voice. Gina maybe? And the words, "You have the right to an attorney."

Turning off the phone, she leaned her head back against the wall and closed her eyes.

"Did they check you out already?"

She opened her eyes and peered at Nash.

Milena should be the one the police were arresting, for surely admiring someone as good-looking as Nash had to be a crime. She swallowed down her emotions, Because feeling them meant becoming vulnerable in his presence.

She had opened herself up again.

If she had pain, it came from welding back together the severed ties between them.

He pulled her to her feet, coaxing her in for a hug.

Milena sank into his embrace, knowing she shouldn't enjoy being this close to him. She felt his heart beating next to her ear, and it did strange things to her—things she hadn't wanted to feel again.

Out of all the people in her life at this moment, Nash had become her pillar.

But she had to let him go.

He had a life that no longer involved her.

"What do you say we get out of here? Just you and me."

She thought about it. Thought about what would happen once they walked out of these doors. About the white mermaid dress she'd bought. Dreams. Secret desires.

And she no longer wanted to play the part of a pawn.

Milena shook her head. "I plan on leaving as soon as I've had word on Ivan."

"You're still sticking around for him?"

"I need to know if he's okay. I get it if you don't understand."

She had a terrible history with the men in her life. As she'd sat there for the past hour, she decided she could forgive Ivan. He had just as much been a victim in all this as she had. Deep down, she wanted to believe his and her father's betrayal was justifiable. Still wrong. Still painful.

And maybe one day her mother would forgive her. It had been the right thing to do. She'd called Gina in Nash's absence and told her everything. Some things the newspapers hadn't known.

"I think I do." Nash held onto her. "You care about

people. You care about him. I was afraid none of us would get out of there."

"Why did you come to the office if my father didn't send you?"

He pushed back a strand of her hair. "You don't think after the meeting at the Oyster House I could walk away and not come back, did you? Not after all we'd been through."

"I appreciate that."

He tilted her head up so he could capture her lips with his. He kissed her with a gentleness that made her want to weep with the beauty of it. He explored, tenderly, letting her know there was so much more for them to come if she was willing to go there.

He smiled against her lips. "I like where this is going."

"Too bad I won't be able to stay." She cringed at her own words, turning her face to the side and pressing her cheek against his heart.

"Excuse me. Are either of you here for an Ivan Yaroslav?"

Milena pulled back. She turned to address the woman in dark blue scrubs. "I am."

The nurse tucked an iPad under her arm and said, "He's in recovery. It will be a few hours before they assign him to the ICU. The bullet nicked a lung. If you want to see him, you'll have to get clearance with the authorities. Officers have been assigned to his room."

"Thank you," Milena sighed.

"They won't let you see him, at least for a while."

"I know. I suppose it is time for me to go."

"I'll take you. Where do you want to go? We never got to finish our lunch at the Shake Shack."

She pressed her hand against his heart, tilted her head in. How much had changed in such little time?

"I've already called for a ride to take me to the airport."

———

"Airport?"

Her words smacked him in the soul like an unexpected punch. There was no other way to ease the pain.

"I can't stay here. After everything that happened. I can't."

She spoke regarding her parents, her ex-fiancé, and his chest felt no less battered by her walking away from him.

Those people in her life who were to be the most trustworthy were the very ones who made her life the most complicated.

She glanced at her phone. "I should call Gina and tell her I'm ready to go."

Nash drew back, looking her up and down. "You called Gina?"

"I've caused you enough trouble. Gina was more than happy to assist me."

She squeezed his arm and walked out of the waiting room.

With these thoughts in mind, Nash couldn't let Milena go.

On impulse, he ran after her, catching up to her as she made it through the sliding front doors. Nash grabbed hold of her and whirled her around. "Just where do you think you're going?"

"Far. Far. Away from here," she said.

"Then I'm coming with you."

He yanked her against him, held her in a hug. She held

herself tense against him. "Go home, Nash. It's over. My father. Ivan. Anton. It's done. The police can sort the rest of it out. Callahan is probably in a tizzy over all this not going in his favor."

"Who is Callahan?"

She took a deep breath. "The man who took your phone. The CEO of Boyko is working with my father."

"I'm glad you got that cleared up and I'm happy to let the police take care of the rest. I wonder how your mother will take all this."

"She knows my wedding to Ivan is off. I'm not sure which has upset her more, the canceled wedding or the officers who showed up at her door to escort her to the police station."

Nash raised his hands to her shoulders. "I'm sorry about your upcoming nuptials."

Although it thrilled him, he could see the shell shock of the past few hours taking over her system.

"I had already told my father I wouldn't marry him. My mother never could take no for an answer. I suppose someday I might have a use for the dress, and the cake will freeze."

She had a dress. The cake. And the church.

Nash couldn't help the wide smile spreading across his face.

"Ever eat cake after it's been frozen for a long time? It would be a shame to ruin a perfectly good cake like that. What you might do is wear your dress, and we could eat that cake together after we go through with the ceremony."

She stepped out of reach, and instantly he missed the feel of her in his arms. He had tried to give her space in the past. Too much space. He wouldn't let her go far from him again this time.

"I told you. There will not be a ceremony. Ivan's going away. If not to prison, he'll return on his visa to his family in Russia."

"Who said anything about you marrying Ivan?"

Milena lifted her head and met his gaze. He wished he knew what she was thinking, but those thick lashes over her eyes hid them from him. She kept her thoughts to herself, and it was killing him.

He tried to phrase it in another way, hoping she would catch on. "You've got the dress, the cake, and the place all set, right?"

"I do."

She could say those words to the priest when they got married.

"All you need is a groom." He held out his arms.

"You?"

He tried not to look as affronted as she'd wounded him. "Would that be so bad?"

"You want to marry me?" she asked.

"I would have asked you sooner if your father hadn't sent me packing, and I hadn't been nursing my pride for so long. I love you, Milena. Wherever you go, I go. Whatever you do, I'll be there supporting you, no matter what."

She blinked and he could see the moisture on her lashes. "And my father's companies?"

"He can have them," Nash said. "You can start your own company, go work for a company, or not work at all. I don't care. All I want is you."

She sniffled. "Not work at all?"

He shrugged. "Between the dogs and the kids, you might not want to work outside of our home."

"I suppose if I take you, I have to take your dog, too."

"And kids?" He might have been pushing it a little far.

"I believe those are negotiable."

He grinned, lopsided, and was filling fast with joy.

"Soo…" She was killing him with the delay.

"How do you feel about alligators and beachfront properties?" she asked.

"Great. My parents have been talking about retiring to Florida for years. Bryon and Jaylene have been talking about getting a place together when they marry, so they can take over the lease on mine. See, we're all good. Marry me, Milena?"

Oh, baby, say yes. Nothing had ever felt this right in his life as it did right this moment.

"I have a dress. A smoking hot one, if I do say so." She tapped her lips. "I could give the cake to Bryon and Jaylene. After all, they showed up at the restaurant, most likely for you."

"For both of us. They both know how much you mean to me."

"This will be interesting to explain to Father Hendrix."

"Milena," he practically growled.

She laughed.

"You don't want my father's company or his money?"

"He will need it for the lawyers to straighten out the mess he's gotten himself into with Callahan and your mother."

Her smile, addictive, spread wider. "My friend, Alysa, has to be my maid of honor. She's also going to be my business partner for our new online tracking app for when you lose things."

"I'll be the first one to sign up." Nash moved closer to her, put his hands on her waist, drawing him to her. "I have to have some way to keep track of you."

Her laugh went clear to her belly, real and raw, and sent

spirals of giddiness growing between them. This time she pulled his head down, slanted it at just the right angle. Her fingers caressed his cheek. "Then I suppose I'll have to marry you. You said you'd follow me anywhere."

"Is that the only reason?"

"I love you, too, Nash."

"Now that, my love, I believe."

Sounds of sirens approaching the hospital grew louder as she kissed him, holding them both to their word.

SNEAK PEEK! RECKLESS HEARTS
CHAPTER ONE

"Marah, you got a call on line two, and Doc Harrison needs that suture done at bed twelve."

Marah finished securing the sling on little Reggie Blake's arm. Poor kid had a black eye and a set of cracked ribs.

Mom stood on the other side of the bed brushing back Reggie's cowlick. He tilted his head trying to avoid her touch.

Marah went about her business. She felt for the kid, and she understood how young boys had a brain to do stupid things. "All right, you all. Hang tight, and we'll get those discharge papers, Mom."

Mom nodded, a few stray tears trickling down her pale face. Marah had no doubt eight-year-old Reggie had taken at least a dozen years off his momma's life. She pointed at him. "And don't you come back now. You hear?"

Those eyes glazed with the onset of pain killers, and exhaustion looked so solemn at her; it nearly broke her heart.

A rustle of the curtain and a shout from Gail, she said to Reggie. "No superman off the roof anymore, promise?"

"Okay." Reggie glanced at his mom.

Mom nodded in agreement. Marah squeezed Mom's arm as she headed out. "Suture in twelve!"

"I've got it. You get that phone. Sheriff Brady ain't going to stay on that line forever, girl."

Marah's chest squeezed close. Lengthening her stride, she made her way to the nurses' station. Bending over the counter, she grabbed the phone. "Sheriff."

"Marah. It's your momma."

"I'm on my way." She slammed down the phone, turned, and found Dr. Harrison in her way. His stout frame made it easy for him to block her. "Running off again, Marah?"

Dr. Harrison reached behind her, and she didn't have to look to know that Kim had turned to hand him a can of Coca-Cola.

Trying hard not to react to the sound of the tab cracking open as he took a swig and arched his brow at her, Marah said, "I'm sorry. It's Momma. I've got to go."

"And I've got a patient in bed twelve waiting to have the cut between his toes sewed shut."

"I've got it," Gail walked past, holding up the suture kit.

"Thanks, Gail." Marah side-stepped out of the way, grateful the words she had been thinking hadn't escaped her mouth. She needed this job. Needed it enough to put up with Dr. Harrison and his Coke-drinking, potato chip-greased fingered bedside manner. She'd once heard him tell a patient not to eat the very thing he stood in front of the man chopping down on. It had taken everything she had not to let him hear her laugh. And she had, at the nurses' station with the other nurses away from his ears.

She'd shake her head later. No wonder the man's wife left him.

No time. Marah had to get to Momma. What could it be now?

"You'll make it up to me later," Gail called back.

Dr. Harrison narrowed his eyes at her as Marah slipped out from between him and the nurses' station. "You'll need someone to cover your shift."

Marah glanced at her watch, relieved by the time, "Janet will be coming in less than an hour."

Dr. Harrison made a noise in his throat. At the sound of his name, he turned on his heel and headed down the hall.

Taking this opportunity to slip away, Marah practically ran from the emergency room. Her heart pounded, thinking of what could have happened this time. She grabbed her purse and jacket and was on her way.

The last thing Marah had said to her brother was to stay home, watch Momma, and she'd call later to check on them.

Did he listen?

Of course not.

Myles had the patience of a rabbit and the mind of a mule. One day it would get him in trouble, but that day wasn't today.

Marah prayed, hoping her brother had enough sense not to have run off when he knew someone had to stay with Momma. It was bad enough she had to take all the evening and night shifts to give Myles daytime hours to attend school.

She never bothered locking Momma's old sedan in fear the lock would catch as it had a habit of doing and not open when she tried. She could make the drive home blind if needed. With one headlight brighter than the other, she pulled out of the hospital parking lot and made the twenty-five-minute drive home.

As she turned and headed down the old dirt road leading to their farm, a sickening feeling stirred deep in her belly. It had been almost ten years since the accident that took her older brother Mark's life, but every time she drove over the spot, it was like walking across his grave.

As she got closer to the farm lane, she turned off her headlights. Lights glowed up the road in the trees.

What was Tyler Evens up to?

No one had been up to that old hunting cabin in years.

Trying to ignore the tightening of her gut, Marah drove past the barn and parked out by the old machine shed. A police SUV sat near the house. She no more than got out of her car when the front door opened, and Momma stepped out on the porch followed by Sheriff Brady.

Momma stood in her pearl snap housecoat and an old pair of Daddy's socks. "I called the police. I told them they were trespassing!"

"I'm sorry, Sheriff." It was all Marah could think to say to him.

Sheriff Brady pulled back his shoulders and rested his hands on his hips. "There's no one here, Marah."

"I know." Marah reached out to take Momma by the arm. "Come on, Momma."

"They're up there again. They're messing behind our barn." Momma pointed out behind the house.

"The barn's on the other side of the lane, Momma. Where's Myles?" Marah asked.

Sheriff Brady let his shoulder sag as she stepped out of her way to take Momma back in the house.

"Didn't you see the lights? They're up there; up to no

good. Something bad is going to happen. I'm telling you they got no business up there. Your father built that cabin."

And Momma went on and on as Marah got her in her recliner. She put the blanket over Momma's legs. Marah clicked on the television, and Momma went quiet, switching her attention to the late-night game show.

Marah put the remote in her mother's hand and squeezed it. "You watch your show, Momma. Don't you worry about it. Ain't nobody up there or around the barn. It's okay."

Then Momma gazed over at Marah, bending over the chair. "You stay away from that Evan boy, hear? It's bad enough your brother went running off again with that boy. Nothing but trouble."

"I know, Momma." Marah's heart squeezed. Behind her, Sheriff Brady cleared his throat. She straightened, took a deep breath, and went into the kitchen, leaving Momma to her late-night show. Marah hoped the show would distract Momma enough to help her fall asleep. Where was Myles?

She was going to kick that younger brother of hers to the next county if he didn't start getting his head on straight. She dropped down into a chair at the table. Her purse slid down from her shoulder to the floor.

At least she'd almost made it to the end of her shift before the call came.

"This is the third time this month, Marah." Sheriff Brady stood, arms crossed, and used the same stern voice with her as he had when she was in high school. His brows drew together. "Now, you're gonna have to do something about your momma."

"I'm sorry Momma called and disturbed you, Sheriff."

Sheriff Brady's eyes softened. "It's not the calls that

bother me, Marah. I can't keep driving out here for false calls."

"I know. She's lonely is all, and sometimes she forgets." Marah hung her head. "Myles is supposed to be here. I don't know where he is." Anger burned down her throat and in her gut. At that moment, she could hear a truck coming down the lane. Leave it to Myles to pick a time like this to show up.

"I'll go drive around, probably just Tyler and some buddies drinking around the bonfire up at the cabin on a Friday night."

Marah swallowed hard and nodded. It felt like a lifetime ago when her older brothers, Matt and Mark, used to invite their friends up there to hang out. How long had it been since she ventured on that side of their property?

"Sheriff, don't you be afraid to cuff those boys of mine when you see them. They know better."

"Oh, I will," Sheriff Brady called out to her, raising a brow at Marah. He tilted his head toward the door, and she followed.

A truck pulled in the driveway; in the dark, it was hard to make it out, but it had dual wheels and her brother Myles drove the old Ford F-150.

As the truck parked and the cab lit up with the door opening, Marah froze on the porch. She blinked to let her vision adjust in the dark, her stomach curling as the light-haired man stepped away from the truck.

"Is that who I think it is?" it came as barely a whisper.

Sheriff Brady adjusted his hat and looked out across the yard to where the pole lamp sent an eerie glow across the grass.

"After your mother called us at the station, she decided

to venture up to the cabin on her own. Tanner Evans found her walking down the road near his granddaddy's lane."

Marah's throat tightened.

Tanner?

Her chest tightened.

Tanner Evans?

It couldn't be.

"You mean Tyler."

"No. Tanner, the younger of the two," Sheriff Brady said.

But that would mean?

Her lungs held all their air, and she managed to squeak out. "What's Tanner doing here?"

The world would spin shortly.

Tanner Evans?

She felt the sting deep in her chest, tried to force out air to breathe again.

"He said he had an errand to run and would stop on his way back to check on Penny."

That couldn't be right. Momma got things mixed up all the time, but the Sheriff?

Oh no. Not Tanner.

Please, Lord, he wasn't ever supposed to come back.

A wad of grief and a decade-old ache erupted from around her heart. She tilted forward a little, tried to keep her lungs from shutting off.

"You gonna be alright?" Tanner stuffed his hands in his pockets and walked up the front steps.

Now that was the billion-dollar question of the night.

Marah tried not to let the sheriff see the wave of nausea swelling inside her. Her heart beat faster as to nudge her lungs to get working back to normal again.

Nothing was ever normal around here anymore. And it wouldn't ever be with Tanner Evans back.

If it was Tanner.

She gritted her teeth looking at the devil himself. At first, she could have mistaken him for Tyler, the two brothers had similar features, but as he came closer under the porch light, there was no mistaking him.

Tanner Evans had returned.

"I take it you can handle things from here." Sheriff Brady squeezed her shoulder and went down the stairs. He gave Tanner a long look at which both men seemed to come to a silent understanding.

She wanted to scream, to shout, for Sheriff to stay. Why was he leaving her when he knew what Tanner had done? Why wasn't he arresting him and taking him far away from here?

"I wasn't sure if you'd be home yet," Tanner said, smooth and calm as ever while every fiber in Marah's being held taut as she found words to respond. "As you can see, I'm here."

And a dozen different emotions she'd been holding inside her started to crack open. She had nothing to say to him.

For years, she'd tried to put the memories behind her. Forget Tanner. Forgive what he'd done to her—not her, but her brother Mark.

"Your mom okay?"

"She's fine. She gets confused sometimes." Marah said, grateful when Tanner did not attempt to come up the stairs. He stuffed his hands in his pockets and rocked back on his boot heels. Maybe Momma had been right calling the sheriff. A man like Tanner out this late at night, running errands, had to be up to no good.

By the look of the dark shadow on his chin and his hair cropped a bit shorter than she remembered, there wasn't much else that had changed about him.

"I figured. She wandered over near the creek by our place, and I've found her a few times up by the cabin. I've brought her back more than once. Usually, Myles is here."

It struck her like a paper cut, the pain sharp and quick, causing her to suck in her breath.

Tanner Evans had found Momma?
Had she been going to his farm?
Had he been here before?

"Yeah, he is. Usually."

Hearing the game show on the television inside the house and her chest getting tighter, she bit her lip against the sickening feeling that had started in her stomach.

Tanner was the reason her brother Mark was dead. How on earth was she supposed to be okay?

She glanced at her watch. It was almost eleven o'clock.

"I'd best be getting home. Milking comes early. I'll see you around."

She hugged herself, watching him walk away.

She waited until the truck pulled out of the yard and the lights headed toward the Evan's Dairy Farm to sit on the step and bury her face in her hands.

When the cold set in her bones, Marah went back in the house; Momma didn't sleep much at night anymore. She couldn't blame Myles for falling asleep if he'd been here at all. She sat and watched *The Price is Right* until she heard the truck pull in the yard well past midnight.

Marah gritted her teeth, glancing back at Momma and then got up to greet the tall, lanky man who stepped inside the kitchen door.

If looks could kill, she would have had Myles pinned against the wall in a flash.

The silence stretched as Marah fought to push her anger down. She'd let it brew since Tanner left.

Myles took one look at her and muttered a curse.

"Watch your mouth; Momma's awake."

Myles peeked in the living room. "She's always awake this time of night."

"Which is why you're supposed to be here with her." Marah glared harder at him. "Where have you been?"

"Mark, is that you?" Momma called from the living room.

Myles moved past her to the doorway and said, "No, Momma, it's Myles."

Then Momma went back to her show. Marah stood with her hand on her hip, and her anger churned from a low-grade burn to full fury.

Myles turned with his hands up. "Don't even go there, Marah."

"Where were you? It's past midnight! I had to leave my shift early. Do you know what that means?"

"So, you left early." Myles shrugged. "Unlike you, some of us have a life." Myles walked into the living room.

"We have a deal. You go to school during the day and stay with Momma at night while I work."

"No, Marah. You're the one who said I would stay with Momma at night. I have a life, and it ain't stuck on this farm."

"You sound just like Matt." Marah glanced over at Momma, her eyes drifting off to sleep as if her children weren't standing in the same room with her yelling at each other.

"Why do you think I work nights so you can go to

school during the day? Do you think I like working the night shift? Or twelve hour days sometimes? I do it for you and Momma."

"Well, nobody asked you to." Myles headed for the stairs.

"Myles?" Momma was wide awake.

"Yeah, Ma?" He said, not bothering looking back.

"It's past your bedtime. You need something?" Momma asked.

"I'm good, Momma." Myles headed up the stairs.

Marah sighed. A hand reached out and touched her arm. "You out with that boy again tonight? It's about time you got home."

There was no sense in arguing. "I'm home, Momma. Don't you worry. I ain't going anywhere."

SNEAK PEEK! RECKLESS HEARTS
CHAPTER 2

Every morning was the same old story. Tanner stretched with a cup of steaming coffee in hand, sending a curl of white mist from the lip of his travel mug as he made his way from the house to the barn. Old Matilda bawled, and the other cows moved restlessly inside the barn. A peek of the sun bled over the pastures, through the trees with golden hues and red highlights of autumn making its mark.

Tanner yawned, he could have done for at least another hour of sleep, having been up most of the night checking on one of the heifers about to freshen. Poor thing had been showing signs of labor for two days.

He had started chasing her in from the pasture late last night when he found Mrs. Lehman out on one of her wanderings. She'd gone with him when he found her out in the dark.

She chatted away, in her motherly fashion, as if nothing had ever happened between her family and his all those years ago.

His gut twisted, and not from Pap's black wake up juice.

His brother, Tyler, leaned against the milk house with his hand stretched out. "Pap said there would be frost in the morning."

Tanner gave him the vicious brew their grandfather concocted every morning and called it coffee. "Things are bound to warm up around here sooner or later."

"Is that so?" Tyler took a sip of his coffee and winced. "You know when you got back, you said you were sticking to the farm, but then you were out pretty late last night. What's her name?"

"Dora."

"Where she from?"

"She's one of ours. I had to chase her in from the pasture last night before she dropped her calf out in the field. You can find her and little September in the far back pen in the barn."

"Wait." Tyler held up his hand. "You named the calf September? Serious man?"

"Born in September, named it September."

Tyler shook his head. "You need a life. You're getting as bad as Pap naming those animals."

He had a life, a long time ago, when he'd been young and stupid. He thought long and hard about coming back to Hidden Hills, and couldn't think of anywhere else he'd go. He'd tried to prepare himself for all the changes, but not much had changed. Especially Marah. After all these years, she looked as pretty as she did back in high school.

Rather than dwell on what was and what couldn't happen, he changed the subject. "Where did you go last night? I could have used your help chasing in that heifer."

"Out at Luke Myer's place, welding new blades on Ben's old plow. He busted two, and Luke had an older model up in his equipment graveyard. I stayed until about ten then came home to crash. Four a.m. comes early," Tyler held up his coffee.

"So, you weren't up at the old cabin?"

"On the Lehman place? I wouldn't be caught dead there." Tyler flinched, he reached up and pulled down his knit cap over his head. "I didn't mean—"

Tanner waved if off. "No big. Mrs. Lehman claimed she heard someone up there. She was out last night, and I found her when I went to retrieve Dora."

"Ain't that like the second time you've been over there?" Tyler narrowed his gaze.

"Third."

"You think that's a good idea?"

"What did you want me to do? Leave her out wandering the woods at night?"

"I can't say I wouldn't have done the same thing. You see, Marah?"

"Yeah."

Tyler sat his cup of joe on his truck hood. "You're alive, so?"

"So, Mrs. Lehman called the sheriff."

"How did that go?" Tyler asked.

"I left as soon as the sheriff showed up. I figured it was best, and I had to see to Dora since you weren't around. I stopped back to check on her and figured Myles would be there, but it was Marah."

"Bet she was happy to see you."

From inside the milk house, Pap shouted. "Cows ain't gonna milk themselves."

"I guess that's our call to get a moooove on," Tyler chuckled at his lame joke and tipped up the coffee to his lips. Tanner shook his head and moved past him.

Marah had seemed anything but happy to see him. Not

that he could blame her, bad blood between them and all. He tried to get her out of his head. Spent years trying not to think of her or that moment when he'd see her again. Not that it mattered much. There wouldn't ever be anything between them.

The night he wrecked Mark's Pontiac Grand AM had sealed their fate.

He breathed in the crisp air of grain and manure. He listened to the hum of the compressor warming up, and it grounded him back to reality.

"The fence out in the back forty near the Lehman's place is down again. After we get cleaned up here, I'll need you to give me a hand. Maybe you could ride up to the cabin and take a look around. I doubt the sheriff went up there, seeing as Mrs. Lehman gets confused sometimes."

"I wouldn't think you'd want to go back there. It's probably a bunch of teenagers having a kegger."

"Which is why someone needs to make sure no one ever gets hurt up there again."

Tyler's response was drowned by the sound of the compressor kicking on in the milk house. Its loud buzz calling the herd as they shuffled and shoved in the waiting pen. If they didn't get the first batch of cows in the stanchions soon, Pap would curse them up a storm for all the milk going to waste. Tanner rolled the sleeves of his flannel shirt to his elbows and went to bring the cows in.

Down in the pit of the milking parlor, a wrinkled and white bushy-haired man stood scowling at them both. "Can't keep the ladies waiting for you boys; let's get a move on. We've got a day of chores ahead of us."

"Maybe he does," Tyler bumped Tanner in the arm.

Tyler whistled as he took the steps to the pit. He sat the

travel mug on the top of the cement stairs and grabbed the washrag, rolling back his shoulders, "Let'm in."

It took a little over two hours to milk them all, switching six cows on each side. Tanner did the washing, Pap swinging the milkers, and Tyler filling the feeders and swapping the cows through the chutes. At the end of leading the last bunch of cows back out, Tyler had slipped outside to feed a few calves and disappeared.

He could hear the rumble of the diesel engine as Tyler left for work. Farming had never been in his older brother's blood. Tyler's talents were in his trade of welding.

Inside the milk house, the sounds of the compressor shut off, and Pap stepped out, wiping his aged hands in a rag before tucking it in the back pocket of his pants. He grunted and pointed a gnarled finger. "Long night. You catch some z's before you try working on that fence. We don't need no accidents around here."

"No, Pap. No accidents."

"Tyler." His grandfather shouted.

"He's gone already."

Pap's face scrunched up. "Don't you forget to clean out the back pens." Then Pap shuffled his way past Tanner toward the old farmhouse. "Bacon, be ready in a bit."

And he knew better than to argue.

The scent of Pap's burnt bacon and fresh farm eggs in the morning had been a welcomed aroma compared to the powdered eggs, and processed stuff served in prison.

He might have served his time, but people wouldn't ever forget.

Either way, he'd lost his best friend that day.

He didn't think Mark's sister would ever forgive him.

He'd seen most of the Lehman's since coming home six

months ago. It was kind of hard to avoid them being in a small town like Hidden Hills.

Not feeling hungry, he headed around toward the machine shed.

"Breakfast is in the other direction," Tyler said, stepping out of the milk house.

"I heard the truck. I thought you left."

"I parked it behind the barn. I need to unload those new gates for out in the back forty. I am off today, so I thought we could get that done before Pap started harping on us."

"I'm taking the four-wheeler out to check the fence in the heifer field. I'll meet you there in a couple of hours. We might as well work our way forward."

"You sure about this?" Tyler asked.

"Somebody's got to fix it. Those new gates will be the least of our worries if a cow gets loose and wanders over to the Lehman's."

"True. But we don't want Pap having a heart attack either." Tyler punched Tanner in the shoulder. "Take your cell phone with you."

Tanner patted his front pocket. "Always."

Inside the machine shed, Tanner checked the gas and pulled the four-wheeler. He took the fence line and followed it around the pasture that connected his grandfather's land to the Lehman's.

Not far out, he spotted a maroon SUV going down through the woods. He sat and idled, watching it leave the direction of the cabin. Taking out his phone, he snapped a quick picture.

Driving farther up the pasture and away from the vehicle, Tanner parked it near the broken fence and went to inspect the section. They had recently replaced the posts;

he and Tyler had put them in not long after his release, and they'd strung up new wire.

Tanner picked up the end of a broken strand.

It wasn't electric, but the high-tension wire strung between the posts had been cut, and Tanner slipped his phone back in his pocket. He walked through the opening in the fence and into the woods. He spotted the roofline of the cabin. Smoke curled from the chimney.

ABOUT THE AUTHOR

Growing up on a farm in Pennsylvania, Susan Lower yearned for adventure. A woodsy gal, Susan prefers camping over going to the beach any day. Still a farm girl at heart, Susan writes fast action reads filled with cowboys, heroes, and hope. She writes both western historical and contemporary romances, romantic suspense, and has been itching to one day write a mystery or thriller. Christmas is her favorite holiday, and she loves to write resilient characters struggling to overcome the complications of life while holding their values and strengthening their faith.

Sign up for Susan's newsletter at susanlower.com, where you'll get free books, exclusive bonus content, and news of her releases and sales.

READ MORE BY SUSAN LOWER

SILVER WIND EQUINE RESCUE ROMANCES
Forgotten Reins

Unbridled

Silver Stirrups

HEARTS OF HIDDEN HILLS SERIES
Residence of Her Heart

Savaged Hearts

Reckless Hearts

BRIDES OF ANNIE'S CREEK
The Fruitcake Bride

The Thimble Bride

The Postage Stamp Bride

www.ingramcontent.com/pod-product-compliance
Lightning Source LLC
Chambersburg PA
CBHW020110180626
46812CB00006B/2551